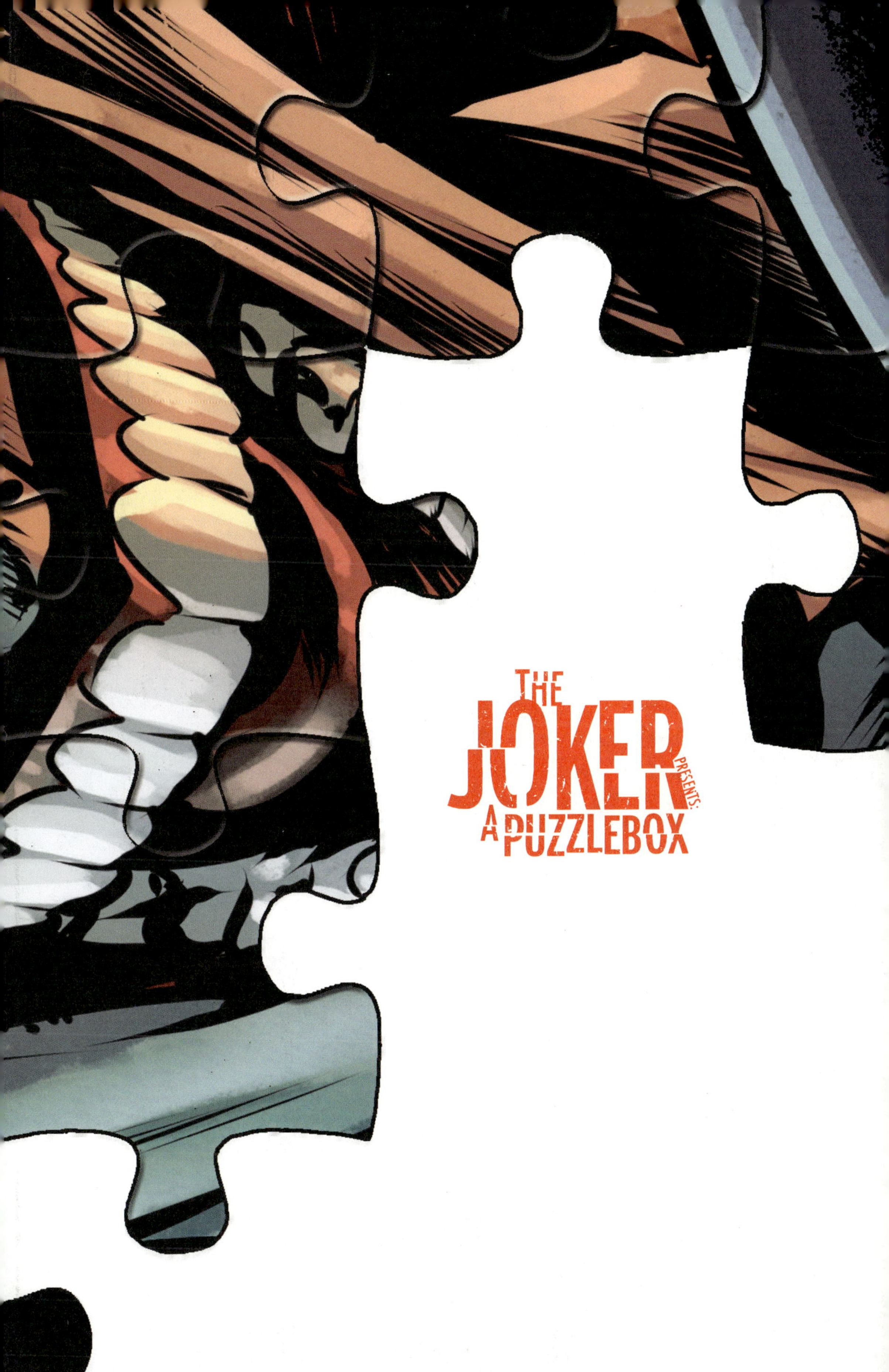

THE JOKER PRESENTS: A PUZZLEBOX

THE JOKER PRESENTS: A PUZZLEBOX

MATTHEW ROSENBERG
writer

JESÚS MERINO · JOSHUA HIXSON
KERON GRANT · DANI · VICENTE CIFUENTES
DOMINIKE "DOMO" STANTON · JUNI BA
VANESA DEL REY · RICARDO LÓPEZ ORTIZ
CHRISTOPHER MOONEYHAM · FREDDIE E. WILLIAMS II
SHAWN CRYSTAL · JUAN DOE · MIKE NORTON
artists

ULISES ARREOLA · JOSHUA HIXSON
KERON GRANT · JEROMY COX · MIKE SPICER
NICK FILARDI · EVA DE LA CRUZ · TONY AVIÑA
ROMAN STEVENS · JUAN DOE
colorists

FERRAN DELGADO
letterer

RYAN BROWN
collection cover artist

BATMAN created by **BOB KANE** with **BILL FINGER**.
SUPERMAN created by **JERRY SIEGEL** and **JOE SHUSTER**.
By special arrangement with the **JERRY SIEGEL FAMILY**.

KATIE KUBERT Editor – Original Series & Collected Edition **LIZ ERICKSON** Associate Editor – Original Series
STEVE COOK Design Director – Books **DAMIAN RYLAND** Publication Design **CHRISTY SAWYER** Publication Production

MARIE JAVINS Editor-in-Chief, DC Comics

ANNE DePIES Senior VP – General Manager **JIM LEE** Publisher & Chief Creative Officer
DON FALLETTI VP – Manufacturing Operations & Workflow Management **LAWRENCE GANEM** VP – Talent Services
ALISON GILL Senior VP – Manufacturing & Operations **JEFFREY KAUFMAN** VP – Editorial Strategy & Programming
NICK J. NAPOLITANO VP – Manufacturing Administration & Design **NANCY SPEARS** VP – Revenue

THE JOKER PRESENTS: A PUZZLEBOX

DC Comics, 100 S. California Street, Burbank, CA 91505
Printed by Transcontinental Interglobe, Beauceville, QC, Canada. 7/15/22. First Printing.
ISBN: 978-1-77951-662-6

Library of Congress Cataloging-in-Publication Data is available.

The Joker Presents: A Puzzlebox #1 cover by **CHIP ZDARSKY**

THE JOKER PRESENTS: A PUZZLEBOX
CHAPTER 1: Step into the Box
MATTHEW ROSENBERG writer
JESÚS MERINO, JOSHUA HIXSON artists
WHY DON'T YOU TELL US WHAT HAPPENED?
YOU ASKED IF ANYONE WOULD TALK TO YOU, I SAID YES, AND YOU BROUGHT ME INTO THIS ROOM THAT, FRANKLY, SMELLS A BIT LIKE URINE AND HAS A VERY CONSPICUOUS MIRROR.
CAN I GET SOMETHING TO EAT? I DIDN'T FINISH MY CAKE.
IF YOU TALK.
THAT'S ALL I EVER DO, LIEUTENANT.
BATMAN created by BOB KANE with BILL FINGER.
ULISES ARREOLA, JOSHUA HIXSON colorists
FERRAN DELGADO letterer

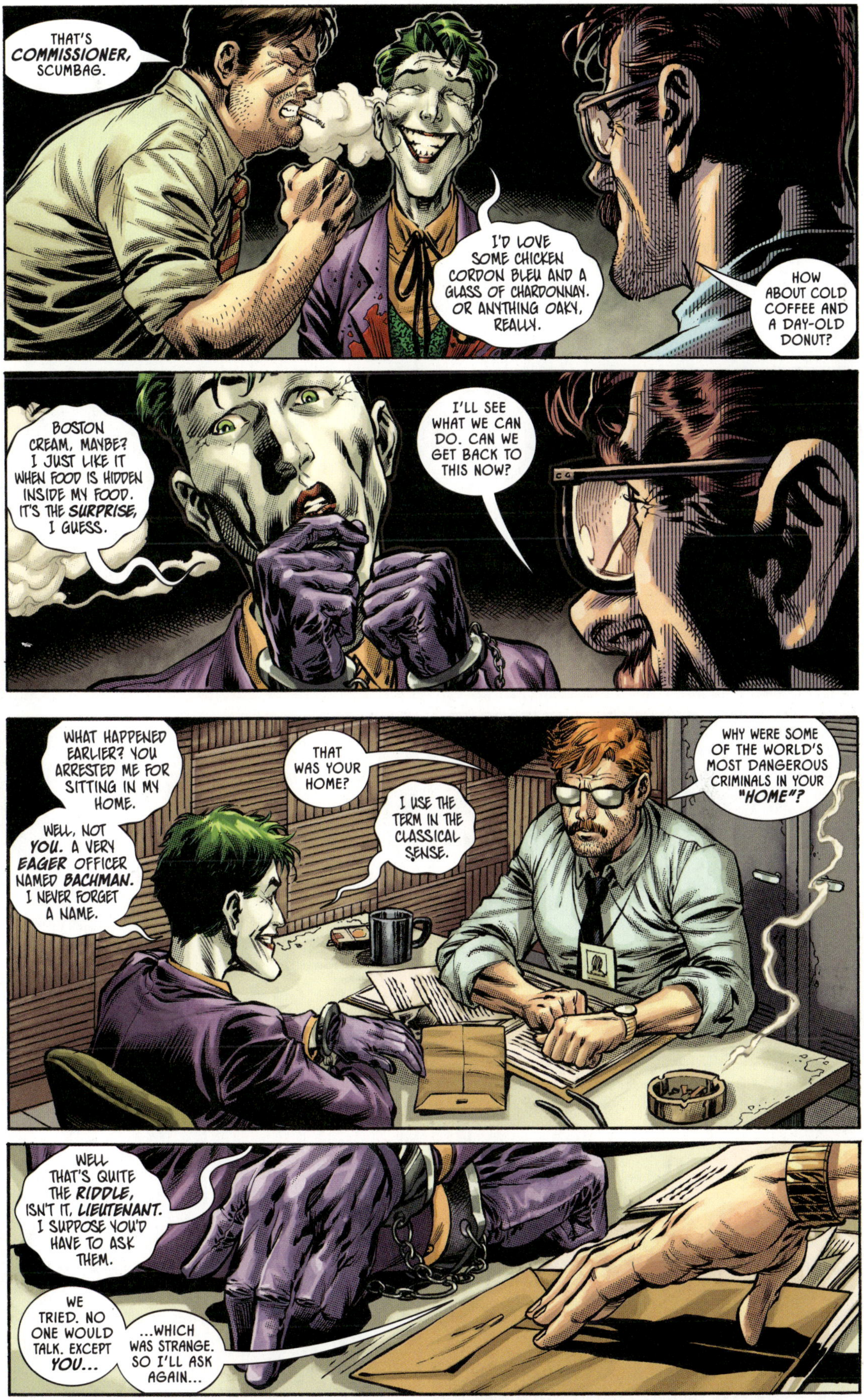
THAT'S COMMISSIONER, SCUMBAG.
I'D LOVE SOME CHICKEN CORDON BLEU AND A GLASS OF CHARDONNAY. OR ANYTHING OAKY, REALLY.
HOW ABOUT COLD COFFEE AND A DAY-OLD DONUT?
BOSTON CREAM, MAYBE? I JUST LIKE IT WHEN FOOD IS HIDDEN INSIDE MY FOOD. IT'S THE SURPRISE, I GUESS.
I'LL SEE WHAT WE CAN DO. CAN WE GET BACK TO THIS NOW?
WHAT HAPPENED EARLIER? YOU ARRESTED ME FOR SITTING IN MY HOME.
WELL, NOT YOU. A VERY EAGER OFFICER NAMED BACHMAN. I NEVER FORGET A NAME.
THAT WAS YOUR HOME?
I USE THE TERM IN THE CLASSICAL SENSE.
WHY WERE SOME OF THE WORLD'S MOST DANGEROUS CRIMINALS IN YOUR "HOME"?
WELL THAT'S QUITE THE RIDDLE, ISN'T IT, LIEUTENANT. I SUPPOSE YOU'D HAVE TO ASK THEM.
WE TRIED. NO ONE WOULD TALK. EXCEPT YOU...
...WHICH WAS STRANGE. SO I'LL ASK AGAIN...

"...WHY WERE THEY IN YOUR HOME?"
"THEY WANTED TO THROW ME A THANK-YOU PARTY."
POPCORN
YOU SHOULDN'T HAVE.
"THANK YOU FOR WHAT?"
CLAP! CLAP! CLAP! CLAP! CLAP! CLAP! CLAP!
"YA KNOW... THEY NEVER SAID. AND I DIDN'T ASK."
JOKER, YOU FUN MANIAC!
TIME TO PARTY!
"ASK TOO MANY QUESTIONS AROUND PEOPLE LIKE THESE AND YOU'RE LIABLE TO END UP DEAD."
"I'M KIDDING, OF COURSE. BUT IT DIDN'T MATTER."
DID IT JUST GET EXTRA DARK IN HERE OR...?

"BECAUSE YOU-KNOW-WHO SHOWED UP.
SMASH!
"AT FIRST I THOUGHT THEY'D HIRED SOMEONE TO DRESS UP LIKE THE BAT, BECAUSE WHAT'S A SURPRISE PARTY WITHOUT SURPRISES...
PLAF!
"...BUT THEN I REALIZED YOU'D HAVE TO BE TRULY CRAZY TO DO SOMETHING LIKE THAT.
"IT WAS REALLY HIM. THE FURIOUS RODENT IN ALL HIS AUTHORITARIAN GLORY."
"BATS AREN'T RODENTS."
"YES, YES. MAMMALS OF THE ORDER CHIROPTERA. I ALSO KNOW HOW TO READ, LIEUTENANT."
HE'S MINE!
TIME TO GO, BOYS!
WHAP!

"AS MUCH AS HE IS AN EMBARRASSMENT TO THIS AMAZING CITY, ITS WONDERFUL PEOPLE, AND ITS ADEQUATE LAW ENFORCEMENT...
"...THE BATMAN IS A SIGHT TO BEHOLD."
CRAK HAK!
WRAMM!
"AND WHAT WERE YOU DOING AT THAT MOMENT?"
"I WAS ENTHRALLED BY THE SPECTACLE."
I HAVE NO PROBLEM WITH YOU, JOKER. SORRY FOR THE INTRUSION. PLEASE GO BACK TO YOUR CAKE.
THANK YOU, ARNOLD.
"ARNOLD?"
"OH, AWKWARD. ARNOLD IS HIS REAL NAME. IF WE COULD KEEP THAT BETWEEN US I'D APPRECIATE IT."
HOUSE OF MIRRORS
POW!
I WOULDN'T DO THAT IF I WERE YOU, WAYLON.

KZZT!
I TRIED TO WARN YOU, WAYLON. CROCODILES **ALWAYS** LOSE TO BATS.
IT'S THE LAW OF THE JUNGLE.
I'M AN IDIOT.
I KNOW.
FORGET YOU! I'M GOING TO GO HAVE A ROMANTIC EVENING WITH A BIRD.
WHOK!
I TRIED TO GET WAYLON TO PLAY NICE, ARNOLD.
THANK YOU, JOKER. I **ALWAYS** APPRECIATE YOUR HELP.
I'D BE NOTHING MORE THAN A **VIOLENT JERKWAD** WITH A **BAT FETISH** IF IT WEREN'T FOR YOU.

THIS IS @#$%*!& ABSURD.
SADLY, YOUR SHAVED GORILLA IS RIGHT, LIEUTENANT. IT WAS ABSURD.
THE BATMAN REALLY DOESN'T ALWAYS APPRECIATE MY HELP.
LET HIM TALK, HARVEY.
THIS IS A WASTE OF TIME, JIM, AND YOU DAMN WELL KNOW IT.
THIS IS AWKWARD.
I CAN BRING IN ANOTHER DETECTIVE IF YOU NEED A BREAK, HARVEY.
WHAT I NEED IS TO BE DOING SOME POLICE WORK, NOT LETTING A PSYCHOPATH MAKE UP STORIES--
SHOULD I GO? I'LL GO.
SIT!
OKAY.
YOU AGREED TO COOPERATE WITH US HERE, JOKER.
I AGREED TO TALK TO YOU. THAT'S NOT ACTUALLY COOPERATIVE. I'M MORE OF A MONOLOGIST BY NATURE--
YOU WANNA GO BACK TO THAT CELL?
THEY ALL LOOKED LIKE THEY WERE READY TO HAVE A REAL GOOD TALK WITH YOU.
I AM NOTHING IF NOT VERSATILE. I LIKE TO THINK THERE'S NO ROLE I CAN'T PLAY.
GOOD. LET'S CONTINUE.

THOK!
"NOT MUCH MORE TO SAY. THE BATMAN'S CHILD SOLDIERS ARRIVED...
THROK!
"...AND TRIED HARD TO IMPRESS DADDY.
"AND THEN YOU ARRIVED.
"WELL NOT YOU. ONE ALWAYS SENDS PAWNS IN FIRST..."
"KEEP THE COMMENTARY TO YOURSELF, JOKER. ONE OF OUR MEN WAS SHOT."
"I DIDN'T KNOW. WILL HE BE OKAY?"
"YES."
"TOO BAD."
HANDS BEHIND YOUR HEAD, CLOWN!
THE TALENTED MR. RIPLEY
DID I DO SOMETHING WRONG, OFFICER?
NO! WE'RE ACTING OUT BECAUSE WE HAVE UNSATISFACTORY HOME LIVES AND SUBSTANCE ABUSE PROBLEMS.
I HAVE A PERSONAL GRUDGE AGAINST YOU FOR NO REAL REASON.
I UNDERSTAND. JUST GO EASY ON THE OTHERS. THEY ARE MENTALLY UNWELL.

NOT THE GREATEST STORY EVER TOLD, BUT THAT'S HOW I REMEMBER IT.
IS **ANY** OF THAT TRUE?
ANY WORD ON THAT CHICKEN CORDON **BLEU?**
WHAT ABOUT **HIM?**
WHAT **ABOUT** HIM?
HE DIDN'T COME TO MY PARTY. MUST HAVE BEEN TIED UP WITH--
HE WASN'T AT YOUR PARTY BECAUSE HE'S **DEAD.**
HAHAHA!
HE'S **NOT** DEAD.

WOW.
THESE ARE GREAT SHOTS. DO YOU HAVE DUPLICATES? CAN I KEEP THESE?
WE'RE ONLY GOING TO ASK THIS ONCE, JOKER...
WHO KILLED THE RIDDLER?

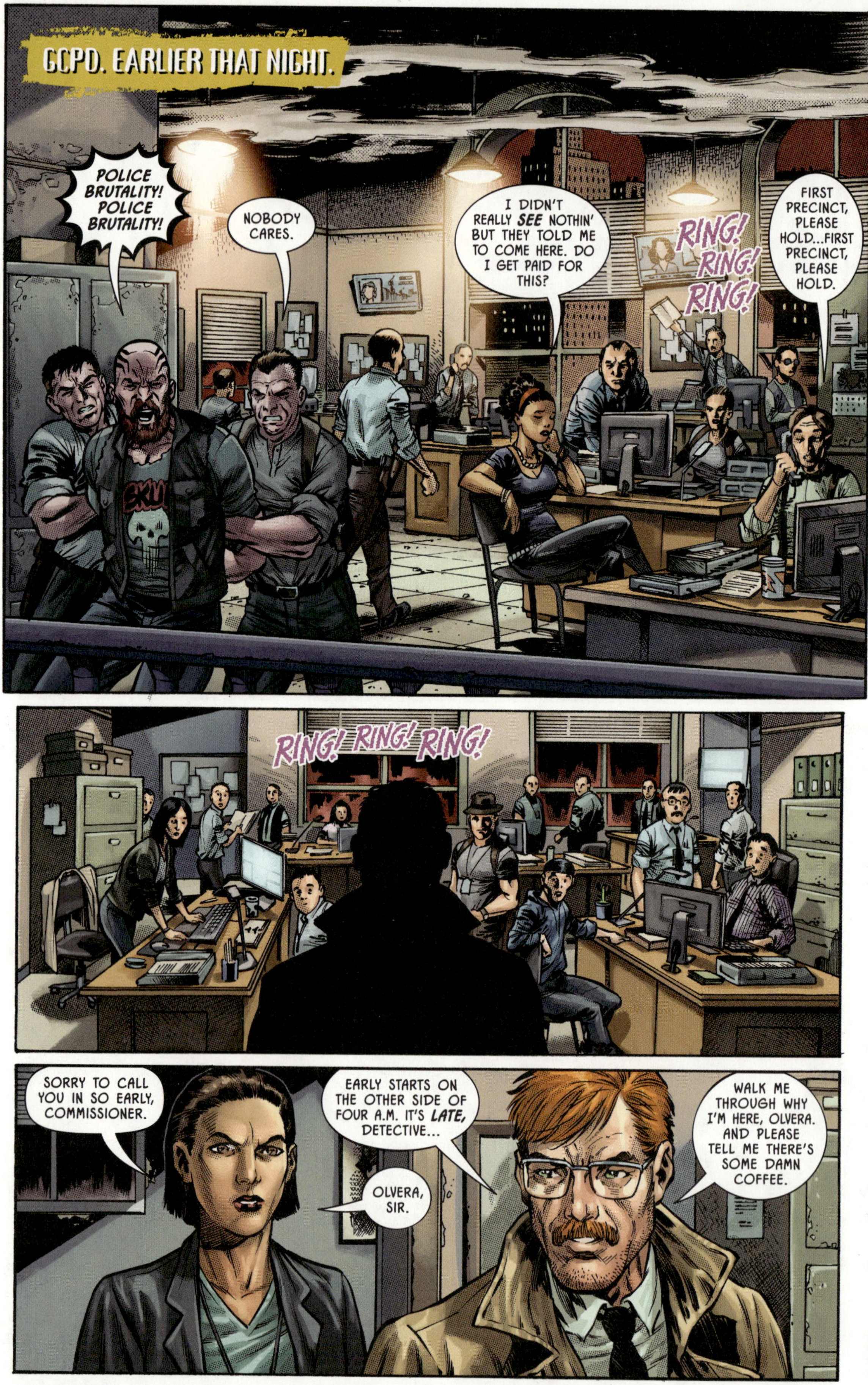
GCPD. EARLIER THAT NIGHT.
POLICE BRUTALITY! POLICE BRUTALITY!
NOBODY CARES.
I DIDN'T REALLY SEE NOTHIN' BUT THEY TOLD ME TO COME HERE. DO I GET PAID FOR THIS?
RING! RING! RING!
FIRST PRECINCT, PLEASE HOLD...FIRST PRECINCT, PLEASE HOLD.
RING! RING! RING!
SORRY TO CALL YOU IN SO EARLY, COMMISSIONER.
EARLY STARTS ON THE OTHER SIDE OF FOUR A.M. IT'S LATE, DETECTIVE...
OLVERA, SIR.
WALK ME THROUGH WHY I'M HERE, OLVERA. AND PLEASE TELL ME THERE'S SOME DAMN COFFEE.

WELL, IT'S A MESS, SIR. SOMEONE LEAKED IT. THE PRESS HAS BEEN RUNNING WILD. WE'RE FIELDING TIPS, THREATS, YOU NAME IT.
CALL IS IN TO THE FEDS FOR ASSISTANCE BUT NOTHING YET.
CAPTAIN ADAMS SAID YOU'D APPROVE O.T. SO ALL OFF-DUTY DETECTIVES HAVE BEEN CALLED IN.
BULLOCK?
HE'S ON HIS WAY, SIR.
THE MAYOR'S OFFICE WANTS TO KNOW WHY HE WASN'T CONSULTED.
SO DO I.
UMM...THE TIP CAME IN LAST-MINUTE. WE DIDN'T WANT TO RISK LOSING THEM. I WAS TOLD THE CAPTAIN SENT SOMEONE TO YOUR HOUSE--
IT'S NOT YOUR JOB TO DEFEND HIS #*$%-UPS, OLVERA.
WHAT ELSE?
I TRIED TO GET A STATEMENT FROM BATMAN AT THE SCENE--
YOU JUST TRANSFERRED TO GOTHAM, EH?
CAN SOMEONE GET SOME FRESH COFFEE GOING IN HERE?
WATCH OUT!
KILL YOU!
SORRY, COMMISSIONER.
NO HARM, NO FOUL.
WHAT'S YOUR FIRST NAME, OLVERA?
IT'S MERCEDES, SIR.
OKAY, I NEED YOU TO CALM DOWN, MERCEDES.
SOME OF US WERE STILL ASLEEP TWENTY MINUTES AGO.

WHERE ARE THEY NOW?
CELL ONE.
WHOSE BRIGHT IDEA WAS IT TO PUT THEM ALL IN THE *SAME CELL?!*
LET ME GUESS-- ADAMS?
HE SAID HE WAS HOPING THEY'D *KILL* EACH OTHER BEFORE PROCESSING AND SAVE US A LOT OF PAPERWORK.
I... I THINK IT WAS A *JOKE,* SIR.
IT WASN'T. BUT IF THEY DO, IT WON'T BE *YOUR* ASS. ANY INTERROGATION ROOMS CLEAR?
EVERY BOX IS OPEN.
THEY AREN'T A *TALKATIVE* LOT, BUT IT'S LIKE THE TREADMILL MY DAUGHTER GOT ME FOR CHRISTMAS-- NOBODY'S GOING TO USE IT, IT'S JUST NICE TO PRETEND.
LOOKS LIKE ADAMS'S WISH MIGHT JUST BE COMING TRUE.
YOU'RE A DEAD MAN!

ALL RIGHT, LISTEN UP!
I KNOW MY ASKING IS PROBABLY A WASTE OF YOUR TIME...
...BUT I THINK YOU'RE ABOUT TO FIND THAT YOU SUDDENLY HAVE A LOT MORE TIME TO WASTE.
ANY OF YOU WANT TO COME TALK TO ME ABOUT WHAT WENT DOWN TONIGHT?
I WILL.
WHO SAID THAT?
HELLO, JIM.

⋞SIGH⋟
OF COURSE.
...OKAY. LET'S GET HIM OUT OF THERE.
AGAINST THE SIDES NOW!
ANYBODY MOVES AND WE WILL LIGHT YOU UP!
JOKER, APPROACH THE CELL DOOR! SLOWLY!
RAT.
SNITCH.
TRAITOR.
MERCEDES, CAN YOU SET HIM UP IN BOX ONE?
THANKS FOR THE PARTY, EVERYONE. IT WAS A WISH COME TRUE.

I WANT MY LAWYER.
LET PYG TALK TO JOKER. PYG WILL MAKE HIM SQUEAL.
I THINK THE JOKER ROBBED ME. GET SOMEONE TO TAKE MY STATEMENT.
WHY IS HE TALKING? IT COULD BE WE TALKING?
YA KNOW HE'S A TOTAL LIAR, RIGHT? LIKE, TOTALLY.
I WANT MY LAWYER.
WHY HAVE I BEEN ARRESTED?
YOU WANNA TALK TO SOMEONE? FINE. I'LL TALK.
YOUR WEAK MIND COULD NOT CONJURE THE TORTURES NEEDED TO MAKE ME SPEAK WITH YOU.
I'D TAKE EITHER OF THEIR LAWYERS.
WHAT'S A GIRL GOTTA DO TO GET HER OWN CELL AROUND HERE?
YOU'LL PAY FOR TRAPPING ME IN HERE.
IF I WERE TO BE RELEASED, IT COULD BE VERY BENEFICIAL TO YOU. IN YOUR INVESTIGATION, I MEAN. OF COURSE.
YOU'RE DEAD, PIG!
...GONNA BE A LONG NIGHT.

GCPD.
DO YOU WANT TO TELL US WHO KILLED THE *RIDDLER?*
IT WASN'T ME.
NOBODY SAID IT WAS YOU, JOKER.
MAYBE YOU SHOULD TAKE OFF THESE HANDCUFFS THEN, OFFICER GORDON?
COMMISSIONER GORDON, CREEP.
NOBODY SAID IT WAS YOU *YET.*
BUT NOW'D BE A GOOD TIME TO TELL US ANYTHING YOU CAN THINK OF THAT MIGHT BE *USEFUL.*
ANYBODY YOU KNOW WHO MIGHT WANT THE RIDDLER *DEAD.*
YOU MEAN BESIDES *YOU* ALL?
CAN YOU THINK OF ANYTHING THAT MIGHT HAVE BEEN A *MOTIVE* FOR SOMEONE TO KILL HIM?
I SUPPOSE MAYBE *THE MASTER ENGINE.*
THAT LITTLE MAGIC BOX...
...THE WHAT?

"...THE RIDDLER TRAVELED THE WORLD LOOKING FOR THAT BOX. A MAN NAMED DR. CARO HELPED HIM."
"IS THIS THE DR. CARO WHO WAS AN ARCHEOLOGIST KNOWN TO WORK WITH KOBRA CULT? HE WENT MISSING RECENTLY."
NOT MUCH FARTHER NOW.
WE HAVE ARRIVED.
THIS IS THE ANTECHAMBER.
INDEED WE HAVE, DR. CARO. BUT WHERE?
SO, NOT OUR DESTINATION. YOU JUST MEANT WE'VE ARRIVED WHERE WE HAPPEN TO BE.
IN · GIRUM · IMUS · NOCT
"ONE AND THE SAME. SCARY PEOPLE TO GET TANGLED UP WITH."
"IN GIRUM IMUS NOCTE."
WHAT IS THAT?
LATIN.
"SO WERE THE KOBRA CULT INVOLVED IN THE RIDDLER'S MURDER?"
BOSS, LOOK! SYMBOLS!
"YOU'RE GETTING DISTRACTED. CAN I CONTINUE?"

SOME OF THE CONJUGATIONS DON'T MAKE SENSE...
"...WE GO IN CIRCLES AT NIGHT"? "WE GO INTO CIRCLES"?
CIRCLE... NIGHT...THE MOON!
WHAT DID THE NATIVE LEGEND SAY WE MUST DO, DR. CARO?
RMMBLE!
"LOOK TO ONE'S SELF BEFORE ASKING OTHERS TO CHANGE." BUT...
BOSS! I GOT IT OPEN.
TO LOOK TO ONE'S SELF IS TO REFLECT.
SHK
SHOULD WE GO IN, BOSS?
FWOO

IN · GIRUM · IMUS · NOCTE
"IN GIRUM IMUS NOCTE... ET CONSUMIMUR IGNI." IT'S A PALINDROME.
WHAT DOES IT MEAN, BOSS?
"WE GO IN CIRCLES AT NIGHT..."
"...AND ARE CONSUMED BY FLAMES."
AARRGH!
FWOOOSH
IF NIGHT ISN'T SAFE, THEN WE MUST TRAVEL BY THE LIGHT OF THE SUN.
LET'S GO.

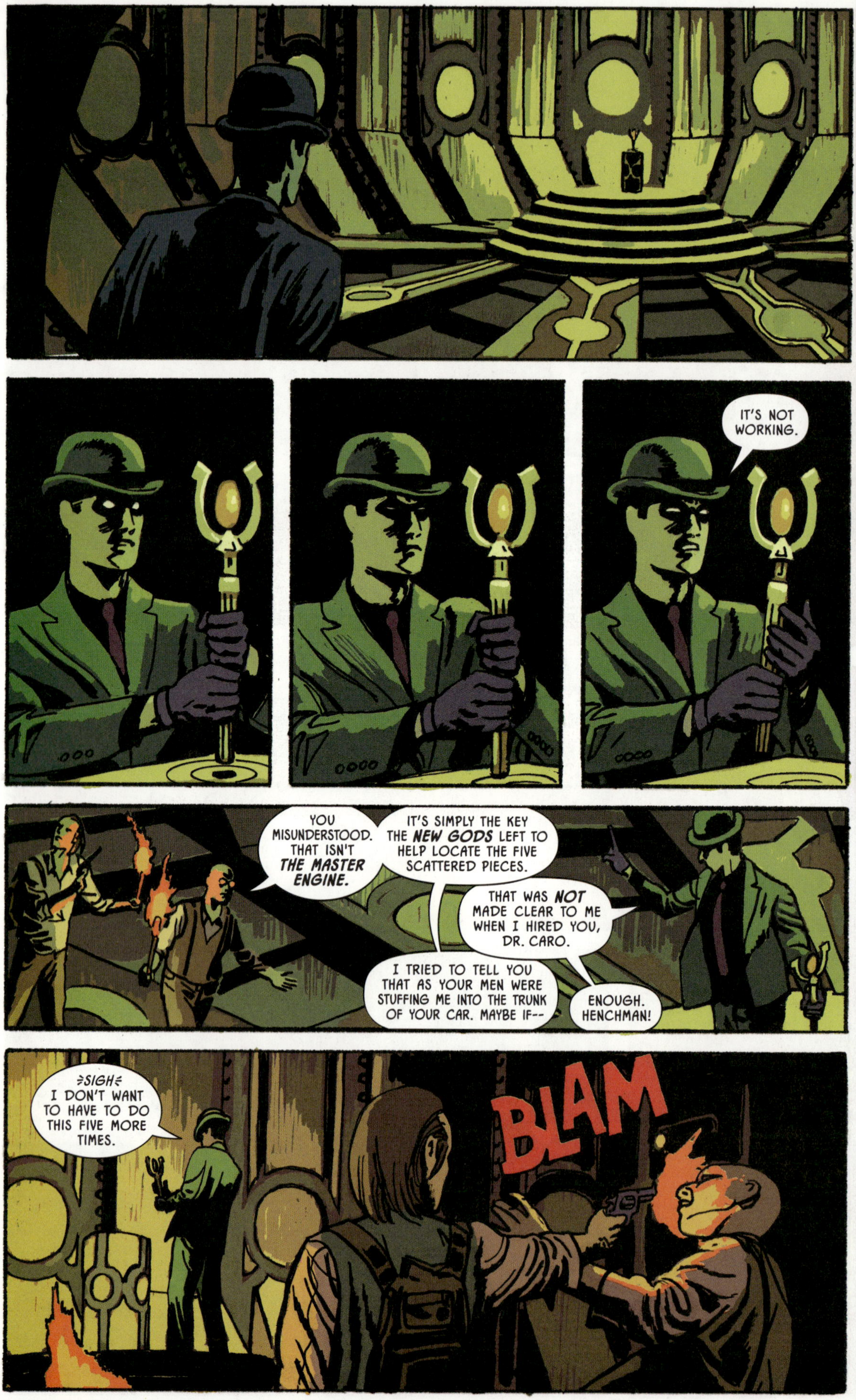
IT'S NOT WORKING.
YOU MISUNDERSTOOD. THAT ISN'T THE MASTER ENGINE.
IT'S SIMPLY THE KEY THE NEW GODS LEFT TO HELP LOCATE THE FIVE SCATTERED PIECES.
THAT WAS NOT MADE CLEAR TO ME WHEN I HIRED YOU, DR. CARO.
I TRIED TO TELL YOU THAT AS YOUR MEN WERE STUFFING ME INTO THE TRUNK OF YOUR CAR. MAYBE IF--
ENOUGH. HENCHMAN!
SIGH I DON'T WANT TO HAVE TO DO THIS FIVE MORE TIMES.
BLAM

A DISGUSTING BASEMENT SOMEWHERE IN GOTHAM.
JOKER, THERE YOU ARE!
WHEN I SAID YOU COULD PICK THE PLACE, THIS ISN'T WHAT I MEANT.
"YOU WENT TO A BOXING MATCH? NO KNIVES? NO CHAINSAWS?"
"YES. BOXING. IT'S A GENTLEMAN'S GAME. AND I AM A GENTLEMAN, COMMISSIONER."
YOU'D PREFER SOMETHING WITH KNIVES OR CHAINSAWS?
BOXING IS A GENTLEMAN'S GAME, EDWARD. PERHAPS IF IT DOESN'T SIT WELL WITH YOU, THAT SPEAKS MORE TO YOU THAN THE SPORT.
I'M SURE THERE'S A CHILDREN'S SPELLING BEE NEARBY IF YOU PREFER.
HA!
WHY IS SHE HERE?
WHY ARE YOU HERE? WHY AM I HERE?
I WANTED TO TALK TO YOU ABOUT MY PROPOSITION, JOKER.
YES, I GOT YOUR MESSAGE. I'M NOT SURE I'M INTERESTED IN DOING BUSINESS WITH A CRIMINAL, EDWARD.

YOU AND I, WORKING TOGETHER? WE COULD DO AMAZING THINGS.
I ALWAYS DO AMAZING THINGS, EDWARD.
WE'VE ALWAYS BEEN CLOSE.
NO, WE HAVEN'T.
SO I GUESS THE REAL QUESTION IS, WHY ME?
MAYBE NOT. BUT WE ARE KINDRED SPIRITS. JOKES ARE JUST RIDDLES FOR STUPID PEOPLE, RIGHT?
SO IT JUST FEELS LIKE WE SHOULD WORK TOGETHER. WE COULD RULE THIS TOWN. WE COULD RULE THE WORLD.
SO IT'S A SENSE OF KINSHIP THEN?
EXACTLY.
SILLY ME. I THOUGHT YOU WANTED TO PARTNER UP BECAUSE YOU ARE OUT OF MONEY, OUT OF HENCHMEN, AND HAVE MADE ENEMIES ALL OVER GOTHAM. BUT THAT'S NOT IT, EDWARD?

YOU KNOW, I HATE IT WHEN YOU CALL ME EDWARD. IT CREATES A DIFFICULT DYNAMIC SINCE NOBODY CAN FIGURE OUT YOUR REAL NAME.
HMM. IF ONLY WE KNEW SOMEONE WHO PRIDED THEMSELVES ON SOLVING THINGS...
IF YOU DON'T WANT TO WORK WITH ME, YOU CAN JUST SAY NO--
NO.
THIS SEEMS LIKE A DANGEROUS GAME YOU'RE PLAYING, WITH POWERS FAR BEYOND YOUR COMPREHENSION.
JUST BE CAREFUL, OLD FRIEND. I'D HATE FOR SOMETHING BAD TO HAPPEN TO YOU.
A WORD OF ADVICE? HIRE FIVE OF THE COSTUMED MORONS FROM OUR CITY'S NEAR-LIMITLESS SUPPLY TO DO THE DIRTY WORK FOR YOU. MAKE IT LIKE A GAME, EDWARD. YOU LOVE THOSE.
THAT'S A @#$%*?& TERRIBLE IDEA.
"WAS THAT THE LAST TIME YOU SAW HIM, JOKER?"
"PERHAPS. I CAN'T QUITE RECALL."
"DO YOU KNOW WHAT HE DID AFTERWARD?"
"YES. HE HAD A BRILLIANT IDEA."

YOU ARE PROBABLY WONDERING WHY I ASKED YOU ALL HERE.
I ASSUME YER PAYIN' US OR YOU WANT TO GET MURDERED BY US...OR **BOTH?**
NO.
POPC
THIS IS WHY!
ARE WE SUPPOSED TO KNOW WHAT THE HELL THAT THING **IS?**
"SO THEY KILLED THE RIDDLER TO TAKE IT?"
"NO..."

THIS THING WILL LEAD US TO MORE POWER THAN WE COULD EVER IMAGINE...
"...AND THEY AREN'T THE INTERESTING PART."
...IT WILL GUIDE US TO FIVE LOCATIONS WHERE WE WILL FIND FIVE PIECES OF A PUZZLE. WHEN ASSEMBLED, THEY WILL CHANGE THE WORLD.
THIS IS ABOUT TO GET FUN, BOYS.
"THEY ARE."

INTERROGATION BOX ONE. GCPD.
THIS IS ALL VERY HELPFUL...
...BUT I'VE RUN OUT OF COFFEE. THIS SEEMS LIKE A GOOD PLACE TO TAKE FIVE.
I CAN GRAB YOU A CUP--
IT'S FINE. I'VE GOT IT, BULLOCK.
COMMISSIONER? I HAVE TO GO TO THE LITTLE BOY'S ROOM! OR THE LITTLE GIRL'S ROOM, IF--
COMMISSIONER! HOW'S IT GOING IN THERE--?
IS ANYONE FROM THE QRT STILL IN THE BUILDING?
I...I THINK SO?
FIND THEM. NOW.

YOU WANTED TO SEE ME, COMMISSIONER?
BACHMAN, RIGHT?
YES, SIR.
YOU WERE PART OF THE QUICK RESPONSE TEAM ON THE RAID TONIGHT?
YES, SIR. MY WHOLE UNIT WAS.
YOU WERE THE FIRST IN?
AH, WELL... *THE BAT* BREACHED WHILE WE WERE GETTING READY. WE DIDN'T KNOW HE AND HIS PEOPLE WERE GOING TO BE THERE.
THAT'S HOW HE WORKS.
IT WAS A MESS INSIDE. I HATE TO SAY IT, BUT IT'S A GOOD THING THE BAT WAS THERE. WE--
ARE THEY STILL ON?
...NO, SIR. WE CLOCKED OUT AT SHIFT CHANGE.
YOU'RE STILL HERE THOUGH. ANYONE ELSE?
KENDLE. SIMS. MAYBE A COUPLE MORE.
I JUST WANTED TO MAKE SURE NOTHING WENT WRONG WITH--
SOMETHING DID.
ROUND UP WHO YOU CAN, *QUIETLY.*

WHAT ARE WE DOING HERE, BACHMAN?
SUITING UP.
I GOT THAT.
I'M JUST ASKING, IS THIS ALL REALLY *NECESSARY?*
JIM GORDON SAYS, "*SUIT UP, WE GOT A THREAT IN THE BUILDING.*"
YOU WANNA TELL HIM **NO,** KENDLE?
NO, SIR.
GOOD. LET'S GO.
PD
CCPD

CAN I...HELP YOU?
THIS AREA IS OFF-LIMITS TO--
BUZZ US IN.
NOW.
CCPD
GCPD
POLICE DEPARTMENT GOTHAM
NOBODY MOVE.
WHAT THE HELL IS THIS?!
ORDERS FROM GORDON. WHERE IS THE EVIDENCE FROM TONIGHT'S RAID?
CCPD
CCPD
BZZZ!
WE'RE STILL CATALOGING IT. WHAT THE @#$% ARE YOU GUYS--
SMAK!
WHERE?!
BACHMAN?

I THINK WE GOT IT.
SECURE THE ROOM.
WE CAN'T LEAVE.
EVERYTHING IN HERE NEEDS DOCUMENTED CHAIN OF CUSTODY--
GET THEM OUT NOW.
HEY!
NOBODY TOUCHES IT. NOBODY GOES NEAR IT.
WHAT DOES IT DO?
HELL IF I KNOW. BUT WE AREN'T GONNA BE THE ONES WHO FIND OUT.
IS IT SUPPOSED TO BE WET LIKE THAT?
Next: BLOOD AND SNOW

CHRIS MOONEYHAN

The Joker Presents: A Puzzlebox #2 cover by **CHIP ZDARSKY**

CLIC!
GCPD.
OKAY, JOKER. LET'S PICK BACK UP WHERE--
AH, CAPTAIN. WELCOME BACK.
IT'S COMMISSIONER GORDON, CLOWN.
YOU PROBABLY WANT TO KNOW HOW THEY FOUND THE BOX, DON'T YOU?
WE WANT TO KNOW WHO KILLED THE RIDDLER.

TAYMYR PENINSULA, RUSSIA.
THE JOKER PRESENTS: A PUZZLEBOX
"THAT'S THE SAME THING."
Blood and Snow, Water and Stone
MATTHEW ROSENBERG writer
JESUS MERINO, KERON GRANT, DANI artists
ULISES ARREOLA, KERON GRANT, JEROMY COX colors
FERRAN DELGADO letterer
BATMAN created by BOB KANE with BILL FINGER
WE'RE ALMOST THERE, SIR.
IT'S ABOUT DAMN TIME.

WHAT IS IT?
LET'S GO.

Slurrp!
THIS IS THE PLACE, BOSS.
YEAH. I GOT THAT.
AND THIS SHOULD BE THE MAN WE CAME TO SEE.
I GOT THAT TOO.
AM I CORRECT IN ASSUMING YOU'RE DIMA?
Slurrp!
DA.
AND I'LL ASSUME YOU KNOW WHO I AM.
DA.
THEN LET'S CUT THE PLEASANTRIES AND GET TO BUSINESS.
YOU HAVE SOMETHING I *NEED*.

<HE IS DISRESPECTFUL, DIMA.>*
*TRANSLATED FROM RUSSIAN.
I DON'T KNOW WHAT THE @#%$ THAT GUY JUST SAID, AND I DON'T LIKE THAT.
THESE @#$%*?!& DON'T SPEAK ENGLISH?
Slurrp!
CAREFUL PLEASE, BOSS.
THESE MEN ARE FORMER RUSSIAN MILITARY. THEY HAVE DONE SOME VERY BAD THINGS THAT MEAN THEY MUST STAY OUT HERE. THEY CAN'T RETURN HOME.
THESE ARE VERY DANGEROUS MEN.
YOU TELL THEM I AM A VERY DANGEROUS MAN.
WE SPEAK ENGLISH.
GOOD. THEN I CAN TELL YOU MYSELF.
I AM A VERY DANGEROUS MAN WHO TRAVELED A VERY LONG WAY TO DO BUSINESS.
WE GOING TO DO THAT OR AM I GOING TO GET ANGRY?
I KNOW WHO YOU ARE, BLACK MASK. YOU ARE VERY DANGEROUS MAN IN GOTHAM CITY, YES?
THIS IS NOT GOTHAM CITY.
NOW WHY DON'T YOU TAKE OFF THAT RIDICULOUS MASK AND WE WILL TALK LIKE REAL MEN.

THE MASK STAYS ON.
AND IF YOU THINK THIS IS THE FIRST TIME I'VE HAD GUNS POINTED AT ME, I'M SORRY TO DISAPPOINT.
BUT I CAN ASSURE YOU IF THIS MEETING DOESN'T GO MY WAY, IT CERTAINLY WON'T GO *YOURS.*
YOU THREATEN ME? *NOW?* YOU ARE A FUNNY MAN. LIKE JOKER.
I'M A *BUSINESSMAN.* I DON'T MAKE THREATS.
I JUST WANT TO MAKE SURE ALL PARTIES UNDERSTAND THE TERMS OF THIS DEAL.
<CAREFUL NOW.>
POINT THAT THING SOMEPLACE ELSE, BORIS.
MY ASSOCIATE MR. BRILL HERE TELLS ME YOU AND YOUR MEN CAME ACROSS AN *ARTIFACT,* SOMETHING NEARLY WORTHLESS TO YOU, BUT WORTH A GREAT DEAL TO MY ASSOCIATES.
I DON'T KNOW HOW YOU GOT IT AND I DON'T CARE.
SO I CAME HERE FOR AN HONEST BUSINESS TRANSACTION.
LIKE A *REAL MAN.*
CAN YOU SAY THE SAME?

"SO BLACK MASK GOT THE PIECES OF THIS 'MASTER ENGINE' BOX THING AND KILLED THE RIDDLER?"
"NO, I DIDN'T SAY THAT...
"...THERE ARE OH SO MANY PLAYERS IN THIS GAME."
HELLO, ROMAN. SEEMS LIKE I MISSED THE PARTY.

I'LL TAKE THAT, THANK YOU.
WOULD YOU MIND CARRYING THE MONEY FOR ME?
OUTSIDE. NOW.
NOT VERY TALKATIVE, ARE YOU?
BLAM!
HOW DID YOU THINK THIS WAS GOING TO GO, ROMAN?
YOU ALWAYS WERE A FOOL.
BLAM!
YOU THOUGHT I FOLLOWED YOU HALFWAY AROUND THE WORLD JUST TO LET YOU SHOOT ME?

DAMMIT. THIS IS TOO HEAVY. WHY DO I HAVE TO DO EVERYTHING MYSELF?
BECAUSE YOU SHOT THE GUY WHO COULD CARRY IT.
SELINA? IT'S HARVEY. CAN YOU HEAR ME?
I GOT IT.
NO, HE WAS NO TROUBLE AT ALL. I'M COMING BACK TO GOTHAM--
BLAM! BLAM! BLAM!
FLUTCH!
SCHIK!
TCHUK!
HARVEY, HARVEY, HARVEY...

...YOU COULDN'T HAVE AIMED FOR HIS HEAD, HARVEY?
POOR MR. BRILL LOOKS LIKE A DAMN MAXI PAD.
YOU... HOW?
YOU THINK I DON'T BRING ANOTHER MASK FOR INSTANCES LIKE THIS?
KEEP IT. A SOUVENIR.
AND I'LL TAKE BACK MY PIECE OF THE PUZZLE.
I'LL LEAVE THE MONEY IN CASE YOU CAN GET A CAB OUT HERE, HARV.
WOULDN'T WANT YOU HAVING TO WALK IN YOUR CONDITION. THAT COULD BE FATAL.
SELINA? I THINK YOU AND I NEED TO HAVE A WORD. DON'T GO ANYWHERE.

SIONIS! LET'S TAKE A WALK!
I'M NOT TALKING TO ANYONE UNTIL MY LAWYER GETS HERE, DETECTIVE ALLEN.
GCPD.
WE CAN'T MAKE YOU TALK, ROMAN. BUT WE CAN MAKE YOU MOVE.
SO MOVE.

BOX ONE OPEN, MONTOYA?
NO, GORDON AND BULLOCK ARE IN THERE WITH THE JOKER.
1
HE TALKING?
LIKE MY GIRLFRIEND AT THE MOVIES.
2
ANYTHING GOOD?
HE SAID OUR MAN HERE FLEW TO RUSSIA AND KILLED A WHOLE MESS OF RUSSIANS.
THAT RIGHT, ROMAN? YOU KILL A BUNCH OF RUSSIANS?
NO COMMENT.
SEE, ME? WHEN SOMEONE ASKS IF I KILLED A BUNCH OF RUSSIANS YOU KNOW WHAT I SAY?
NO?
AND YOU KNOW WHY?
BECAUSE YOU DIDN'T?
YOU'RE DAMN RIGHT.

THIS IS PATHETIC. YOU LEARN THIS WATCHING WIRE RERUNS?
I HAVEN'T BEEN TO RUSSIA IN YEARS. AND I'VE NEVER SHOT ANYONE. CAN I GO BACK TO MY CELL NOW?
I'D REALLY RATHER NOT HAVE PEOPLE THINK I ASSOCIATE WITH THE LIKES OF YOU.
THAT RIGHT, ROMAN? YOU DIDN'T SHOOT ANYONE?
MAYBE WE'LL SEE WHAT TWO-FACE HAS TO SAY.
GO GET TWO-FACE AND PUT HIM IN BOX THREE. WE HAVE SOME QUESTIONS FOR HIM.
YOU THINK ANYONE'S GONNA TALK TO YOU?
IF SOMEONE LIT YOU ON FIRE, THOSE GUYS WOULDN'T $%#@ ON YOU TO PUT IT OUT.
YOU TRYING TO HURT MY FEELINGS HERE, ROMAN?
KEEP ACTING FAMILIAR WITH ME AND IT MIGHT GET PUT TO THE TEST.
YOU'RE RIGHT, ROMAN. THEY DON'T LIKE US.
BUT LET'S FIND OUT IF DENT HATES YOU MORE THAN HE HATES US.

WELL, LOOK WHAT WE HAVE HERE!
THE STAR-CROSSED LOVERS MEET AGAIN.
BUT BOTH ARE FEELING SHY. WHO WILL SPEAK FIRST?
GO @$%& YOURSELF.
DENT WINS.
THAT WAS CHILLY. THAT SEEM CHILLY TO YOU, DETECTIVE MONTOYA?
PRACTICALLY *SIBERIAN.*
YOU GUYS HAVE A FALLING-OUT, ROMAN?
I DON'T TEND TO EVER SEE A PERSON AGAIN AFTER WE HAVE A FALLING OUT.
BECAUSE YOU *KILL* THEM?
BECAUSE THEY'RE SMART ENOUGH TO NOT ANTAGONIZE ME. YOU SHOULD THINK ABOUT THAT.
WANTED
WANTED
2
LAST CHANCE TO FIND OUT WHAT'S BEHIND DOOR NUMBER TWO.
OFFER GOES AWAY WHEN DENT STARTS TALKING.
THIS IS AMATEUR HOUR. TAKE ME BACK TO THE CELL. NOW.

WE'RE TRYING TO HELP YOU HERE. NO ONE'S AFTER YOU.
WE HAVE A BODY AND WE NEED TO FIND THE KILLER AND THE FIRST ONE TO *HELP* US WILL MAKE THEIR LIFE A WHOLE LOT BETTER.
YOU WANT TO MAKE MY LIFE *BETTER?*
PUT ME BACK IN MY CELL OR TAKE THESE CUFFS OFF AND WE'LL SEE WHAT--
PERSONNEL ONLY
I'LL SEE IF I CAN FIND YOU SOMETHING TO EAT AS SOON AS WE GET YOU SET UP, MA'AM.
OH, SORRY. DIDN'T KNOW YOU HAD A SKELL OUT. BOX THREE OPEN?
NO. ALL FULL. YOU CAN TAKE HER TO THE CAPTAIN'S OFFICE FOR NOW.
RIGHT.
NOW WHAT WERE YOU SAYING? IF I TAKE YOUR JEWELRY OFF WHAT ARE YOU GONNA DO TO ME?
LET'S GET THIS OVER WITH.
2

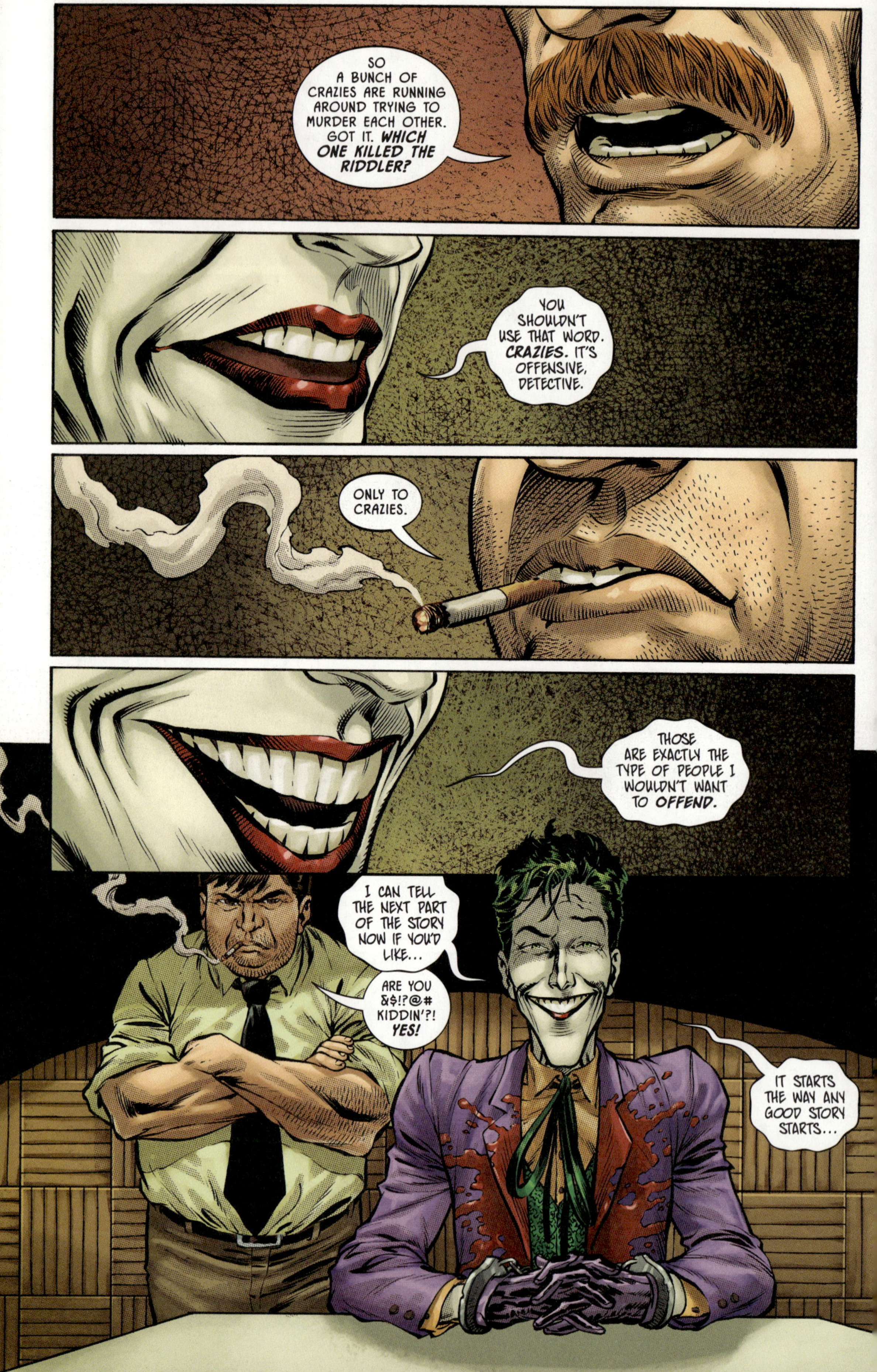
SO A BUNCH OF CRAZIES ARE RUNNING AROUND TRYING TO MURDER EACH OTHER. GOT IT. WHICH ONE KILLED THE RIDDLER?
YOU SHOULDN'T USE THAT WORD. CRAZIES. IT'S OFFENSIVE, DETECTIVE.
ONLY TO CRAZIES.
THOSE ARE EXACTLY THE TYPE OF PEOPLE I WOULDN'T WANT TO OFFEND.
I CAN TELL THE NEXT PART OF THE STORY NOW IF YOU'D LIKE...
ARE YOU &$!?@# KIDDIN'?! YES!
IT STARTS THE WAY ANY GOOD STORY STARTS...

"...WITH A SCARED WOMAN RUNNING FOR HER LIFE."
WHERE DID YOU GO?! COME BACK!
"YOU'RE TELLING US A STORY ABOUT YOUR EX-GIRLFRIEND NOW?"
"PLEASE DON'T REFER TO HER THAT WAY."
"WHAT WOULD YOU CALL HER?"
"A CRAZY."
"AND SHE KILLED THE RIDDLER?"
"PATIENCE..."

HARLEY! STOP RUNNING!
YOU'LL NEVER CATCH ME, YA DISGUSTIN' FREAKS!
AWW, SONUVA...
...YA KNOW WHAT? I CHANGED MY MIND ON GETTIN' CAUGHT.
PAT PAT PAT!
CATCH ME!
NO!

YOU UGLY SACKS O' $#!@ WANT TO KNOW WHERE THIS MASTER ENGINE DOOHICKEY IS?
WE WERE TRYING TO HELP YOU FIND IT!
THOKK!
SO YOU COULD STEAL IT? NOBODY STEALS FROM HARLEY QUINN EXCEPT ME!
"I TAUGHT HER ALL THIS, BY THE WAY."
I DON'T KNOW HOW YOU FOUND ME, YOU CHEWED-UP-BUBBLEGUM-LOOKIN' SWAMP THING WANNABE, BUT I KNOW YOU'RE GONNA REGRET THAT YOU DID.
PLEASE... HAVE MERCY.
NAH.
WHAP!
"I TAUGHT HER THAT TOO..."

THIS IS PROBABLY WHY MY MOTHER TOLD ME NEVER TO GO INTO DARK CAVES ALONE...
...WAIT...
WHY **AM** I ALONE? FEELS LIKE THE KIND OF THING I'D HIRE SOME FRIENDS TO--
HA!
LITTLE GIRL WITH A BIG FROWN.
WHO'S OUT THERE?!
SO SAD WITHOUT HER CLOWN.
IF YOU COME OUT NOW, I **PROMISE** I WON'T BEAT YOUR BRAINS OUT.
PINKIE SWEAR IT. **DOUBLE** PINK--

AHHH!
SPLASH!
BLUB!
GASP!
OKAY, MONSTER. NOW YOU'VE REALLY PISSED ME OFF. SHOW...
ZRRT!
...YOURSELF?

BOLLY?! WHAT HAPPENED?! WHO DID THIS TO MY DARLING GIRLS?!
YOU DID...
NO, I WAS BEING CHASED BY A BUNCH OF SLIMY-LOOKING MONSTERS WHO WANTED TO EAT ME, NOT A BUNCH OF CUTIE-PIE GIRLS WHO WANTED TO SLEEP WITH ME.
I KNOW THE DIFFERENCE. USUALLY.
DON'T YOU REMEMBER? RIGHT AFTER WE ENTERED THE CAVE? YOU FREAKED OUT. SOMETHING MESSED WITH YOUR HEAD...
NOT SOMETHING. SOMEONE.
OH DEAR...
...I SHOULD NOT BE HERE.

MAD HATTER! YOU ***DISGUSTING LITTLE TROLL!*** I'LL SHOW YOU WHAT HAPPENS TO THE TROLLS WHO MESS WITH MY HEAD!
YOU MISUNDERSTOOD! I ***WASN'T*** UP TO NO GOOD!
I ONLY WANTED TO SEE WHERE THE MISSING RELIC WAS HIDDEN. I--
SO YOU COULD ***KILL*** ME AND ***TAKE*** IT!
FAIR POINT, I ***WOULD*** KILL YOU.
WELL, YES. BUT AM I REALLY TO BLAME? YOU'D DO THE SAME.
WAIT! DON'T KILL ME. YOU MIGHT NEED ME TO GET OUT OF HERE!
I DON'T NEED ANYONE, SILLY.
BUT I WANT TO FIND OUT WHO SENT YOU AFTER ME, SO I'M NOT KILLING YOU...***YET.***
YOU'RE NOT THINKING CLEARLY.
I AM NOT THE ONE YOU SHOULD FEAR.
LET'S JUST HOPE I CAN FIND THIS THING BEFORE THE TIDE BRINGS THE WATER IN OVER YOUR LITTLE HEAD, YOU ***DERANGED MILLINER.***
YOU WERE DECEIVED BY MY HAND, BUT IT WAS OPERATING UNDER THE ***CATWOMAN'S*** COMMAND.
RIDDLER SAID THERE'D BE A DANG INSCRIPTION...
...OH, HERE WE ARE...

..."THE WATER IS LOW. IT IS HIDDEN FROM THE EYE. THE WATER IS HIGH."
WHAT THE @#!% DOES THAT MEAN? STUPID RIDDLER. I WISH HE WAS DEAD. I HATE RIDDLES...
...WAIT!
HIDDEN WHEN THE WATER IS LOW...
...THEREFORE, BY THE LAW OF RHYMES, WHEN THE WATER IS HIGH IT WILL...
...IT WILL GLOW!
I LOVE RIDDLES!
GOTCHA!
"FOLLOW HER TO THE CAVES AND ONLY THEN," SHE SAID, "TURN HER AGAINST HER OWN WOMEN," SHE SAID.
WOW. NEAT TRICK.
"WHEN THAT TRAP IS SPRUNG YOU'LL HAVE CAUGHT HER..."

BUT IT WASN'T **MY TRAP** THAT PULLED YOU INTO THAT WATER...
DO YOU HAVE ANY IDEA HOW OBNOXIOUS YOUR RHYMING IS? I SHOULD KNOW. I'M PRETTY @#$%*?& OBNOXIOUS.
BEHIND YOU!
YOU REALLY THINK I'M GONNA FALL FOR ANOTHER OF YER TRICKS? HOW DUMB DO YA THINK--
THROK!
--OOOH. RIDDLER AIN'T GONNA LIKE THAT.
NEITHER WILL THE CAT.

GCPD.
I COULD GUT YOU, MAN.
SETTLE DOWN.
WHEN YOU'RE FINISHED OVER THERE YOU BETTER BE GETTING A MOP.
UM... HELLO?
LEMME GUESS. SOMETHING DRAGGED YOUR NEIGHBOR INTO THE SEWERS?
TAKE A SEAT. WE GOT A LOT OF YOU ALL--
OH...NO, I--
THIS THE "TV SHOWING YOU WEIRD STUFF FROM YOUR CHILDHOOD" THING?
BECAUSE THAT'S A FEDERAL ISSUE. WE'RE SUPPOSED TO SEND YOU--

I'M A LAWYER-- MR. OLIVER.
I WAS TOLD ONE OF MY CLIENTS WAS BEING HELD.
AND I WAS TOLD I HAD TO PAY FOR MY KID'S ACTING LESSONS TO UNLOCK HIS TRUE POTENTIAL. WE ALL CATCH BAD BREAKS.
YOU WANT TO TELL--
I GOT HIM, SERGEANT.
FOLLOW ME, MR. OLIVER.
LATE NIGHT, HUH?
WHEN THE OFFICE CALLS, I DON'T GET TO NOT ANSWER.
IF YOU DON'T MIND ME SAYING, COUNSELOR, YOU ALWAYS SEEMED LIKE A SMART GUY.
YOU COULD GET A JOB WHERE YOU DON'T HAVE TO GET OUT BED AT NIGHT AND COME DOWN HERE TO DEFEND THE SCUM OF THE EARTH.
THANKS FOR THE TIP, OFFICER SAPORTA.
AND JUST SO YOU KNOW, THERE ARE JOBS OUT THERE THAT DON'T REQUIRE YOU TO HARASS INNOCENT AND POOR PEOPLE OR WORK FOR THE MOST CORRUPT POLICE DEPARTMENT IN THE NATION.
HOW'S THE FAMILY?
GOOD. JUST FOUND OUT WE GOT ANOTHER ONE ON THE WAY.
MAZEL.

HE GOT HERE FAST. NONE OF THEM EVEN GOT THEIR CALLS YET.
NONE OF *WHO?*
YOU DON'T KNOW WHAT HAPPENED?
OFFICE JUST TOLD ME HE WAS IN LOCKUP.
OH, YOU'RE GONNA LOVE THIS...
HEY THERE, COUNSELOR. REMEMBER ME?
LITTLE MAN IN A LITTLE MAN SUIT. THINKS HE'S AT THE ZOO.
YOU'RE A LAWYER? GET ME OUT OF HERE. *NOW.*
LOOK AT THE LITTLE MAN IN HIS LITTLE SUIT, TAKING A TOUR OF THE CAGES.
HE THINKS HE'S AT THE ZOO BUT HE DOESN'T KNOW WHY.
COME PET ME, LITTLE MAN SUIT MAN. COME GET IN HERE WITH ME.
GREAT JOB HERE BUT...

"...NONE OF THESE ARE MY GUY."
WHY DON'T WE START AT THE BEGINNING, ROMAN.
BEGINNING OF WHAT, DETECTIVE ALLEN?
WHY WERE YOU IN RUSSIA?
SIGHTSEEING, DETECTIVE MONTOYA.
HEARD THERE WERE SOME SIGHTS...
SO WHAT'S YOUR PROBLEM WITH TWO-FACE?
I DON'T TRUST POLITICIANS.
CUT THE CRAP, SIONIS.
WHO KILLED THE RIDDLER?

THIS IS HILARIOUS. YOU ALL DON'T KNOW ANYTHING, DO YOU?
MAYBE NOT. BUT THE HOMELESS LADY FROM THE HALL... SHE KNOWS SOME THINGS.
SIIIP!
HE SURE SEEMED SPOOKED WHEN HE SAW HER, DIDN'T HE, MONTOYA?
THIS COFFEE'S TERRIBLE. YOU SHOULDN'T DRINK THIS.
SO SPOOKED I THOUGHT HE'D TALK.
TOO BAD, BECAUSE JOKER'S IN THE NEXT ROOM AND HE WON'T SHUT UP.
THAT PSYCHOTIC CLOWN IS A BORN LIAR...
...AND THE FACT THAT YOU ALL ARE TOO @#$%?*& STUPID TO--!
EASY, SIONIS. EASY.
TYPICAL. YOU ROUND US ALL UP FOR A MURDER BUT YOU HAVE NO IDEA WHAT YOU'RE EVEN LOOKING FOR.

SO WHY DON'T YOU TELL, ROMAN?
WE'RE TRYING TO HELP YOU HERE, YOU SMUG @#$&.
BECAUSE I CAN PROMISE YOU JOKER ISN'T DOING YOU ANY FAVORS NEXT DOOR.
TYPICAL GOTHAM COPS. IF THE BATMAN DOESN'T HAND YOU THE CASE WITH A RIBBON ON IT, YOU ARE HOPELESS.
THE RIDDLER WASN'T KILLED BY SOMEONE WHO WAS PLAYING HIS LITTLE GAME. THAT WAS THE GAME.
ALL THE JOKER IS DOING IS MAKING SURE NOBODY CAN TRUST ANYBODY ELSE. AND IF YOU CAN'T TRUST A WORD ANYBODY SAYS, THEN EVERYBODY IS JUST LIKE HIM.
THE JOKER WAS THE ONE--
GOOD EVENING, DETECTIVES.
I ASSUME YOU WEREN'T TRYING TO COERCE ANYTHING OUT OF MY CLIENT AFTER HE REQUESTED HIS ATTORNEY, RIGHT?
YOU CAN STILL TALK WITH US, ROMAN. WE CAN STILL HELP YOU.
MY CLIENT HAS NO COMMENT.
Next: WHO WORKS FOR WHOM?

The Joker Presents: A Puzzlebox #3 cover by CHIP ZDARSKY

GCPD.
GETTING TIRED, CORPORAL GORDON?
IT'S LATE. WHY DON'T YOU KEEP GOING?
SHOULD WE TAKE A BREAK SO YOU CAN CHECK ON SOME OF MY PEERS IN THE OTHER INTERROGATION ROOMS?
WHAT MAKES YOU THINK WE'RE TALKING WITH ANYONE ELSE, JOKER?
YOU WANT TO TELL US WHAT THIS IS?
YOUR DIARY?
CUTE. TRY AGAIN.
WANT A HINT? WE PULLED IT OUT OF THAT WAREHOUSE YOU WERE IN TONIGHT AND WE'RE HAVING SOME TROUBLE CRACKING THE CODE.
WE'LL DO IT, BUT IT MIGHT TAKE A COUPLE DAYS.
YOU BOYS SEEM REAL SHARP. I'M SURE YOU'LL GET IT.
THANKS. MY PARTNER, "SARGE," HERE GOT A GUT FEELING THAT IT'S THE BOOK THAT KEEPS TRACK OF EVERY SINGLE PERSON YOU GOT ON YOUR PAYROLL. AND HE'S GOT ONE HELL OF A GUT.
NOTHING? OKAY, LET'S MOVE ON. WHY WERE YOU IN RUSSIA, TWO-FACE?
SIGHTSEEING.
MUST HAVE BEEN SOME SIGHTS. WE HEARD YOU ALMOST DIED.
SOUNDS LIKE YOU NEED BETTER SOURCES, DETECTIVE CROWE.
WELL WHY DON'T YOU TELL US WHAT HAPPENED?
DID I MISS THE PART WHERE RUSSIA WAS NOW IN THE GCPD'S JURISDICTION?
WE GOT JOKER IN BOX ONE TELLING US STORIES ABOUT YOU.
BLACK MASK IS IN TWO DOING THE SAME--
AGAIN, SOUNDS LIKE YOU NEED BETTER SOURCES.
WE'RE JUST TRYING TO GET YOUR SIDE.

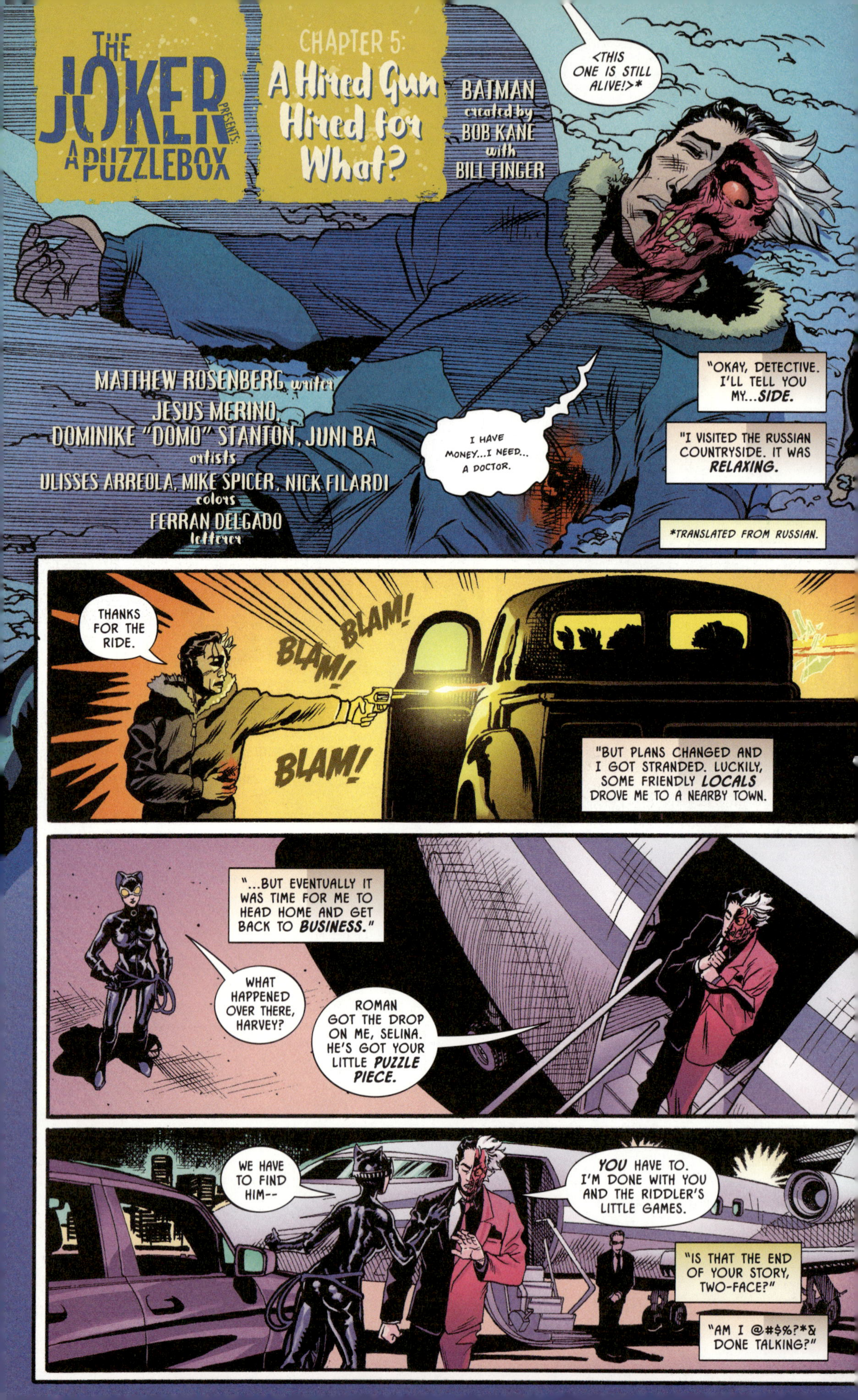
THE JOKER PRESENTS: A PUZZLEBOX
CHAPTER 5: A Hired Gun Hired for What?
BATMAN created by BOB KANE with BILL FINGER
<THIS ONE IS STILL ALIVE!>*
MATTHEW ROSENBERG writer
JESUS MERINO, DOMINIKE "DOMO" STANTON, JUNI BA artists
ULISSES ARREOLA, MIKE SPICER, NICK FILARDI colors
FERRAN DELGADO letterer
I HAVE MONEY...I NEED... A DOCTOR.
"OKAY, DETECTIVE. I'LL TELL YOU MY...SIDE.
"I VISITED THE RUSSIAN COUNTRYSIDE. IT WAS RELAXING.
*TRANSLATED FROM RUSSIAN.
THANKS FOR THE RIDE.
BLAM! BLAM! BLAM!
"BUT PLANS CHANGED AND I GOT STRANDED. LUCKILY, SOME FRIENDLY LOCALS DROVE ME TO A NEARBY TOWN.
"...BUT EVENTUALLY IT WAS TIME FOR ME TO HEAD HOME AND GET BACK TO BUSINESS."
WHAT HAPPENED OVER THERE, HARVEY?
ROMAN GOT THE DROP ON ME, SELINA. HE'S GOT YOUR LITTLE PUZZLE PIECE.
WE HAVE TO FIND HIM--
YOU HAVE TO. I'M DONE WITH YOU AND THE RIDDLER'S LITTLE GAMES.
"IS THAT THE END OF YOUR STORY, TWO-FACE?"
"AM I @#$%?*& DONE TALKING?"

GOTHAM.
"I WENT STRAIGHT HOME TO GET SOME REST."
...UNDER MY SKIN...
"AND THERE HE WAS..."
I HAVE GOT YOU...
CLIC!
YOU COME HERE TO DIE, CLOWN?
HARVEY, HARVEY, HARVEY...
WHY DIDN'T I KNOW YOU WERE A SINATRA FAN?
I've Got You Under My
THIS RECORDING THOUGH... I'VE ALWAYS HATED THIS ORCHESTRA, HAVEN'T YOU?
Scrrrch!

WHAT GAME ARE YOU PLAYING?
YOU SEEM TENSE. DOES THIS MEAN YOUR VACATION WASN'T RELAXING?
I'M NOT GOING TO ASK AGAIN.
YOU MUST HAVE ME CONFUSED. I'M NOT THE ONE WHO PLAYS GAMES. I'M THE ONE WHO TELLS JOKES.
BUT SINCE YOU BROUGHT HIM UP, IT SEEMS THE RIDDLER HAS BEEN MAKING MOVES THAT GOT YOU--
I'VE GOT NO PROBLEM WITH HIM. STOP TRYING TO GET ME INVOLVED IN YOUR FIGHTS.
MY FIGHT? NO, THE FIGHT'S BETWEEN THE CAT AND THE MAN IN THE GREEN HAT.
"I THOUGHT HE WAS TRYING TO ROB ME AT FIRST, BUT IT DIDN'T SEEM LIKE HE TOOK ANYTHING...AT THE TIME."
BUT YOU'RE RIGHT. I SHOULD GO. THE INFORMATION I HAVE WOULD ONLY SERVE TO ANNOY THE RIDDLER AND HAS NOTHING TO DO WITH YOU.
HE WAS SO EXCITED ABOUT WHAT BLACK MASK WAS BRINGING HIM. WE SHOULDN'T INTERFERE...
"REALLY THE CLOWN WAS TRYING TO GET ME TO START A WAR."
...I'M SORRY I BOTHERED YOU.
TALK.

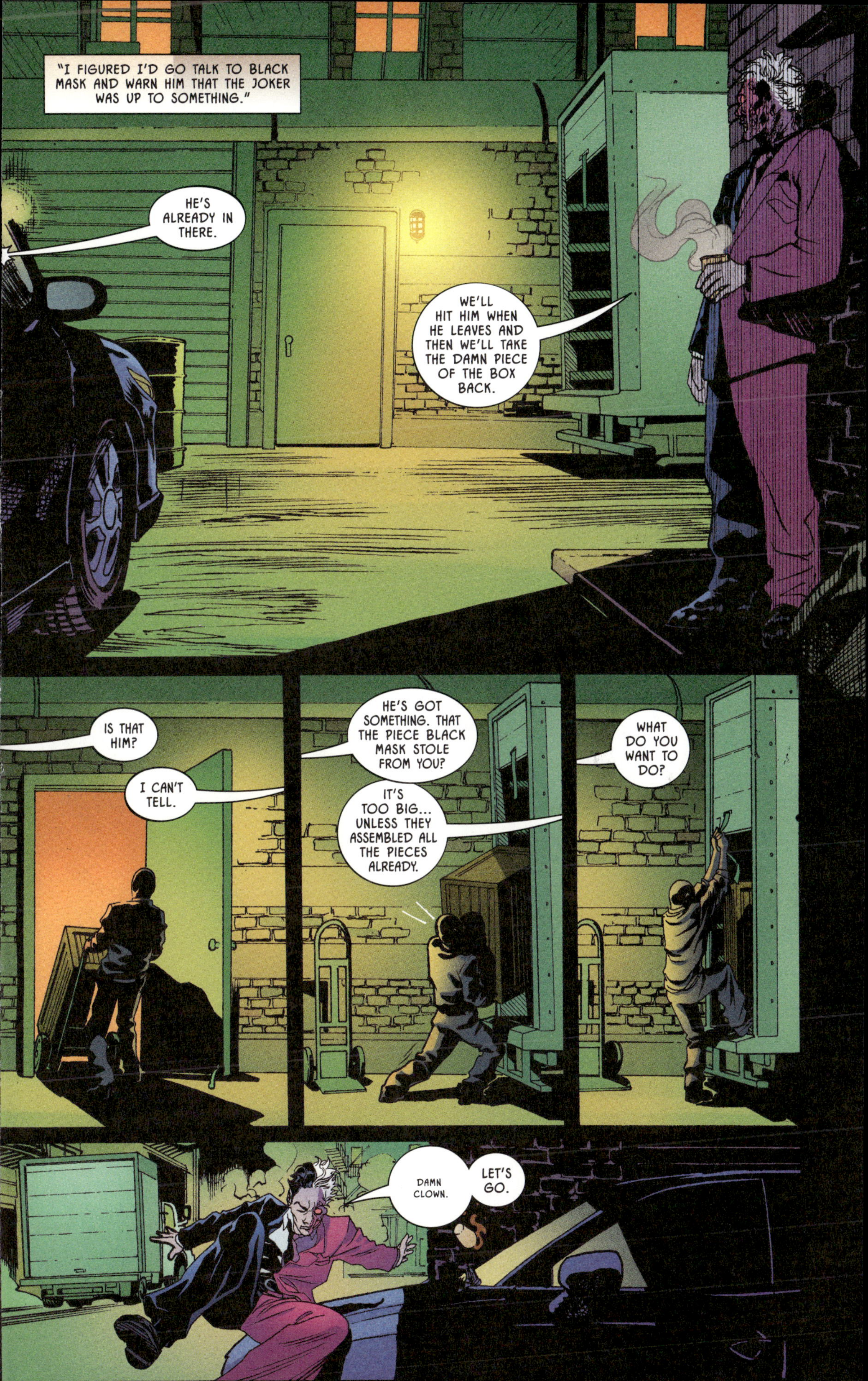
"I FIGURED I'D GO TALK TO BLACK MASK AND WARN HIM THAT THE JOKER WAS UP TO SOMETHING."
HE'S ALREADY IN THERE.
WE'LL HIT HIM WHEN HE LEAVES AND THEN WE'LL TAKE THE DAMN PIECE OF THE BOX BACK.
IS THAT HIM?
I CAN'T TELL.
HE'S GOT SOMETHING. THAT THE PIECE BLACK MASK STOLE FROM YOU?
IT'S TOO BIG... UNLESS THEY ASSEMBLED ALL THE PIECES ALREADY.
WHAT DO YOU WANT TO DO?
DAMN CLOWN.
LET'S GO.

"THE JOKER IS *ALWAYS* UP TO SOMETHING. SOMETIMES IT'S JUST NONSENSE TO AMUSE HIMSELF AND SOMETIMES IT'S SOME GENIUS PLAN.
"BUT IT'S ALWAYS *SOMETHING.*"
"THE TRICK IS FIGURING OUT IF PART OF HIS PLAN IS GOING TO HELP YOU OR HURT YOU.
OH, WHAT THE--
"I WAS WORRIED THAT WHEN I SAID I WASN'T INTERESTED, THE JOKER HIRED SOMEONE TO ROB BLACK MASK.
WHRUNCH!
"SO, LIKE THE *GOOD SAMARITAN* THAT I AM, I INTERVENED."

DEATHSTROKE? ARE YOU KIDDING ME?
LISTEN, MY FIGHT ISN'T WITH YOU.
I'LL JUST TAKE BACK WHAT'S MINE FROM THE BACK OF YOUR TRUCK AND BE ON MY WAY.
WHAT'S YOURS? HA!
WHEN I'M DONE WITH YOU, THE @#$%&* SIDE OF YOUR FACE IS GONNA BE YOUR GOOD SIDE.
TEMPTING. BUT I DON'T THINK SO. DR. PHOSPHOROUS?
THIS ISN'T WHAT I SIGNED ON FOR, DENT.
I MIGHT DO THIS ONE FOR FREE.
"BUT AS USUAL, THINGS WITH THE JOKER WERE MORE COMPLICATED THAN THEY SEEMED."
BLAM!
BLAM!
CHACK!

BLAM!
BLAM!
BLAM!
KRAK!
WHAT THE HELL IS *IN* HERE?
SHOULDN'T HAVE WORKED FOR TWO-FACE, DOC. YOU GET SCREWED EVERY TIME.
BLAM!
BLAM!
BLAM!
FLUTCH!
TCHUK!
SCHIK!

NOW THAT'S NOT FAIR, SLADE.
IT'S ONLY ABOUT **HALF** THE TIME.
WHAM!
OOOF!
BLAM!
BLAM!
BLAM!
WHO WANTS A PIECE OF ME NOW?
THOK!
STAY DOWN.
WRAAMM!

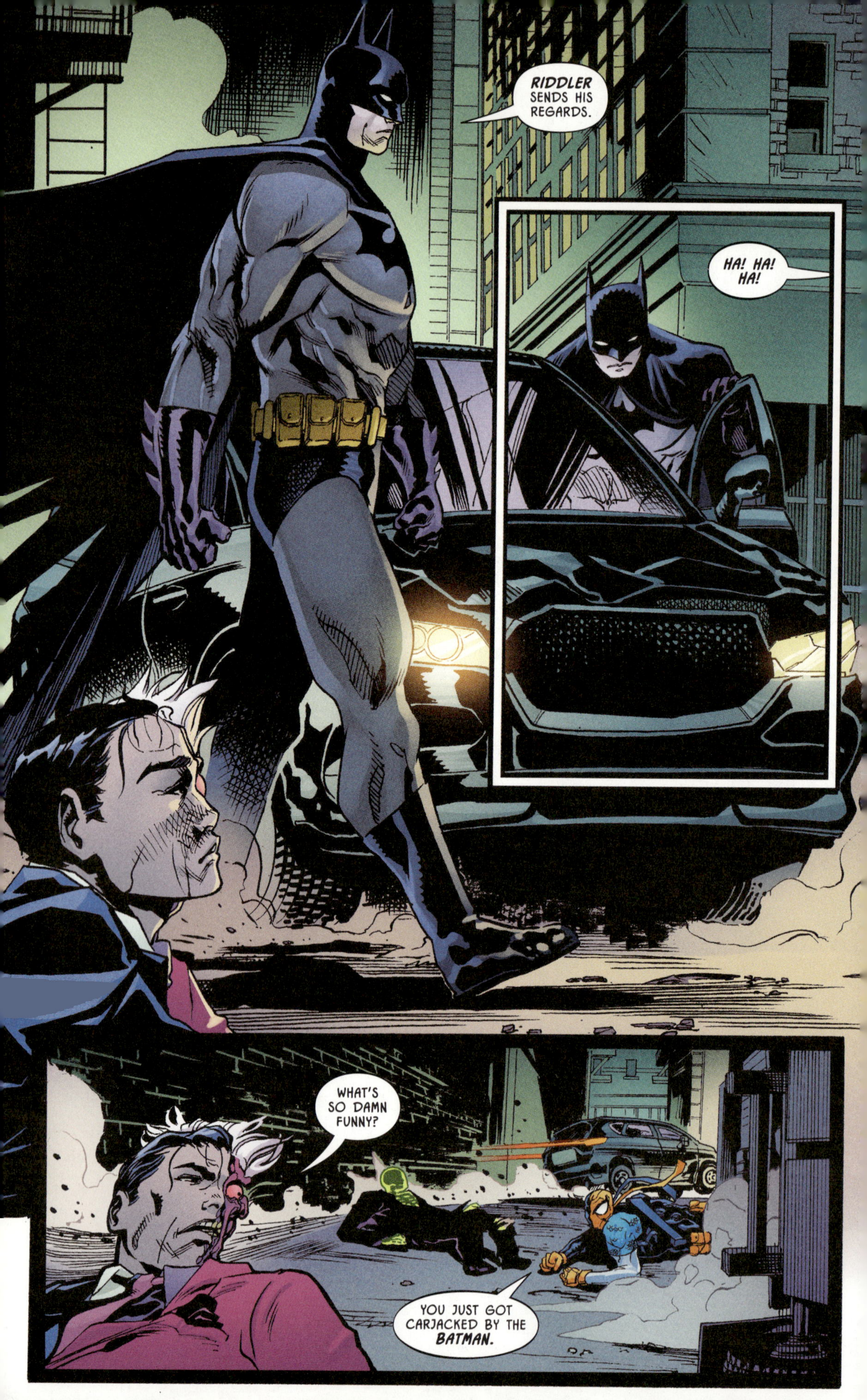
RIDDLER SENDS HIS REGARDS.
HA! HA! HA!
WHAT'S SO DAMN FUNNY?
YOU JUST GOT CARJACKED BY THE BATMAN.

GCPD.
THAT'S A HELL OF A STORY. DON'T YOU THINK, SARGE?
HELL OF A STORY.
THEY STILL GIVE OUT BADGES TO EVERYONE TOO DUMB TO BE A GARBAGEMAN IN THIS TOWN?
YOU'RE LOOKING FOR THE WRONG THING--THE RIDDLER. THE MAGIC BOX... NONE OF THAT MATTERS. THE JOKER IS PLAYING YOU.
WHEREAS YOU ARE THE PICTURE OF A RELIABLE WITNESS.
WE'RE GONNA GO CONFER WITH OUR COLLEAGUES ON THESE SHOCKING REVELATIONS. YOU SIT TIGHT.
HE'S PLAYING YOU!

COME BACK AND LISTEN TO ME, YOU WORTHLESS PIECES OF--!
CLIC!
SOUNDS LIKE IT'S GOING WELL.
GOOD JOB ON THE RAID TONIGHT. WE'D HAVE NOTHING IF IT WEREN'T FOR YOUR TEAM.
YEAH.
ABOUT WHAT YOU'D EXPECT. IT'S BACHMAN, RIGHT?
AND I'D STILL BE ASLEEP IN MY OWN BED.
ANY WORD ON...SINGLEY, WAS IT?
SHE'S STILL IN SURGERY.
WHICH OF THE SCUMBAGS YOU GOT IN THERE ANYWAY?
TWO-FACE. IT'S WHAT YOU'D EXPECT...
...BUT EVEN WITHOUT THE RIDDLER MURDER WE GOT OURSELVES A FEW SOLID WEEKS OF CHASING LOOSE ENDS AND WEIRD LEADS.
OH?
MIGHT HAVE KILLED SOME FOLKS IN RUSSIA. MIGHT HAVE TRIED TO KILL DEATHSTROKE.
DEATHSTROKE? LITTLE OUT OF HIS WEIGHT CLASS, NO?
TWO-FACE HIRED THAT SKELETON GUY TO HELP HIM.
NO, THE OTHER ONE.
NO, THE OTHER ONE.
ATOMIC SKULL?
LORD DEATH MAN?
DIRECTOR BONES?
NO. DOESN'T MATTER.
NOW WE HAVE THIS WHOLE MESS TO DEAL WITH.

WHAT IS THIS?
WE HAVE TO GET IT DECODED BUT MY PARTNER HERE THINKS IT'S A LIST OF EVERYONE ON TWO-FACE'S PAYROLL. IF HE'S RIGHT--
I *AM* RIGHT.
IF HE'S RIGHT, IT'S HUGE.
WHAT HAPPENS TO IT NOW?
WE HAVE TO LOG IT INTO EVIDENCE FOR NOW. WE'LL GO OVER IT WITH GORDON TOMORROW.
UMM... EVIDENCE ROOM IS OFF-LIMITS.
WHAT THE HELL ARE YOU TALKING ABOUT?
MY GUYS SEALED IT TWENTY MINUTES AGO. NOBODY IN OR OUT. NO EXCEPTIONS.
OH, WHO'S ORDERS?
GORDON. SOMETHING DOWN THERE'S GOT HIM SPOOKED.
WELL, TONIGHT JUST KEEPS GETTING BETTER.
I'M GOING BACK DOWN THERE TO RELIEVE ONE OF MY GUYS IN A FEW. YOU WANT ME TO TAKE IT?
NO, WE'LL HANG ON TO IT. EVEN ON DAYS LIKE THIS WE STILL GOTTA RESPECT CHAIN OF CUSTODY.
GET SOME REST, BACHMAN.

GOOD EVENING, MR. DENT.
IS ANYONE WATCHING US RIGHT NOW?
I'D BE PRETTY BAD AT MY JOB IF THEY WERE, WOULDN'T I?
THIS INDICATES TO ME THAT INDEED YOU ARE, OFFICER BACHMAN.
I JUST CAME TO SEE IF YOU NEEDED ANYTHING.
DO I NEED ANYTHING? LET ME THINK.

I NEEDED YOU TO PROTECT MY ASSETS. I NEEDED YOU TO WARN ME THERE WAS A RAID COMING. I NEEDED YOU TO GET ME OUT OF THERE AFTER YOU *DIDN'T* WARN ME. BUT SINCE NONE OF THOSE THINGS HAPPENED...
...I NEED YOU TO GET ME THE HELL OUT OF HERE!
AND HOW WOULD YOU PROPOSE I DO THAT?
GCPD
THEY HAVE MY LEDGER. I DON'T KNOW HOW THEY GOT IT, BUT THEY DID.
I SAW. I TRIED TO GET IT BACK FROM THEM FOR YOU, BUT I COULDN'T.
FOR ME? FOR *ME?* I DON'T THINK YOU UNDERSTAND.
THAT BOOK DOESN'T JUST SCREW ME. WE'RE *ALL* SCREWED, WALTER. *ALL OF US.*

ACTUALLY, MY NAME'S NOT IN THERE.
MY NEW EMPLOYER MADE SURE I'D BE PROTECTED.
WHAT ARE YOU TALKING ABOUT?
YOU'RE DEAD!
YOUR WHOLE FAMILY IS DEAD! EVERYTHING YOU LOVE WILL TURN TO DUST BY MY HANDS, BACHMAN! YOU HEAR ME?
HAVE A GOOD NIGHT, HARVEY.
CLINK!

GCPD.
YOU BELIEVE DENT'S STORY?
I DON'T BELIEVE A WORD THAT COMES OUT OF ANY OF THEIR DAMN MOUTHS.
BUT IF IT'S MY GUY'S WORD AGAINST YOUR GUY IN THERE? SURE. I'LL TAKE MINE.
ARE YOU AND JIM CLOSE, HARVEY? DOES HE EVER HAVE YOU OVER FOR DINNER?
SHUT YOUR MOUTH.
I WISH HE AND I WERE CLOSER. I WAS VERY CLOSE WITH HIS--
WHY DON'T YOU TELL US ABOUT TWO-FACE ATTACKING DEATHSTROKE?
I DON'T KNOW ANYTHING ABOUT THAT.
REALLY? BECAUSE WE HEARD YOU BROKE INTO HIS HOME AND ADVISED HIM TO HEAD TO WHERE THE ATTACK TOOK PLACE.
THAT SOUNDS LIKE THE KIND OF THING I'D REMEMBER, DEPUTY GORDON. WHO TOLD YOU THAT?
TWO-FACE.
WELL NOW, HE'S A LIAR.
FUNNY, THAT'S WHAT HE SAID ABOUT YOU.
NO, I'M A JOKER. HE IS TWO-FACED.
BUT I CAN SEE WHY THAT MIGHT GET CONFUSING FOR YOU.
IT SOUNDS LIKE HE IMPLICATED HIMSELF IN SOME SORT OF CRIME, THOUGH. SCARY.
BUT NONE OF THAT IS WHAT YOU WANT TO HEAR ABOUT ANYWAY. YOU WANT TO KNOW ABOUT THE MAGICAL MASTER ENGINE.
NO. WE WANT TO KNOW WHO KILLED THE RIDDLER.
ONE AND THE SAME, MY LARGE SIMIAN FRIEND. ONE AND THE SAME...

"OUR STORY BEGINS--"
"BEGINS?! YOU'VE BEEN TELLING US STORIES FOR HOURS ALREADY."
"OUR STORY BEGINS WITH A SIMPLE PHONE CALL IN THE FANCY OFFICE OF A SIMPLE MAN."
RING RING
WHAT?
SLOW DOWN. HE'S DOING WHAT?!
STAY ON HIM BUT DON'T TOUCH HIM. I'LL HANDLE THAT.
AND THIS TIME WHEN I TALK TO DENT I'LL MAKE SURE I FINISH THE JOB.
"SO BLACK MASK KNEW TWO-FACE WAS GOING TO ATTACK DEATHSTROKE?"
"I DON'T KNOW. DOESN'T MATTER. THAT WASN'T THE IMPORTANT PHONE CALL..."

BZZ
"...THIS WAS."
SNF SNF
BZZ
HELLO?
SELINA, IT'S--
SOMEONE WHO DOESN'T KNOW NEVER TO USE MY NAME ON THE PHONE. HOW WAS YOUR TRIP?
THE NORTHERN BORDER OF ZAMBESI.
I'M WHERE YOU TOLD ME TO GO... BUT THERE'S A PROBLEM.
I DON'T WANT TO DO THIS. I WAS SURE I COULD BEAT KILLER MOTH HERE AS MYSELF, AND IF THERE WAS SOME SORT OF PUZZLE TO FIND THE ARTIFACT I COULD FIGURE IT OUT...
THERE ALWAYS IS.
MM-HMM...
BUT HE'S HERE NOW. HE'S GOING SLOWLY BUT I CAN'T KEEP UP. I'M NOT GOING TO MAKE IT.
MM-HMM...

WELL, YOU HAVE A WAY OF BEATING HIM, DON'T YOU?
YES, BUT--
AND THAT'S WHY I SELECTED YOU, ISN'T IT?
I KNOW--
I KNOW YOU WON'T LET ME DOWN.
YOU CAN DO THIS. YOU DON'T NEED *HIM.* JUST CLIMB.

CRMBLL!
OOF
HELLO...? CAN ANYBODY HEAR ME...? I'M HURT.
I... MUST...

"A DRUG ADDICT TRYING TO SCALE A VOLCANO, JOKER? THAT'S WHAT YOU'RE GIVING US?"
"IT'S LESS ABOUT THE MAN...
"...AND MORE ABOUT THE ADDICTION."
MAN-BAT TAKES WHAT HE WANTS!
DAMN. YOU'RE BIG.

"SO KILLER MOTH WAS WORKING FOR RIDDLER AND MAN-BAT WAS WORKING FOR CATWOMAN-- IS THAT IT?"
FZZZAK!!
DOESN'T MATTER TO ME.
"YOU ALWAYS SEEK SIMPLE ANSWERS, DON'T YOU? IT'S NOT ABOUT WHO HIRED THEM. IT'S ABOUT WHAT THEY WERE WILLING TO DO ONCE THEY WERE HIRED.
"THESE BOYS? THESE ARE NOT GOOD BOYS."

STOP RUNNING!
STOP TRYING TO EAT ME!
RIPP!
"THEIR SIMPLE ALLIANCES PUT THEM AT EACH OTHER'S THROATS."
OOF
SLOW DOWN, MONSTER. YOU'RE ABOUT TO BITE OFF MORE THAN YOU CAN CHEW.
I DO NOT WANT TO EAT YOU...

...I JUST WANT TO KILL YOU.
WHY SHOULD I? YOU'RE WOUNDED. ALMOST DEAD. I CAN FINISH YOU QUICKLY.
MAYBE. OR MAYBE I'M TOUGHER THAN I LOOK.
YOU DON'T LOOK TOUGH AT ALL.
OH? YOU SHOULD HAVE SAID SOMETHING.
BUT HOW ABOUT THIS? INSTEAD WE WORK TOGETHER.
YOU DON'T LOOK SO HOT YOURSELF. BUT DON'T YOU GET IT? THEY'RE PLAYING US.
CATWOMAN HIRED YOU, RIGHT? PROBABLY EVEN FORCED YOU TO TURN INTO... THIS. RIDDLER HIRED ME.
BUT DO YOU THINK EITHER OF THEM CARES IF WE DIE? THEY JUST WANT THEIR PIECE OF THE MASTER ENGINE.
I WANT IT.
SO DO I. BUT THAT'S MY POINT. THEY SAY IT'S ALL-POWERFUL, RIGHT? IT GRANTS WISHES?
THERE'S NO REASON WE CAN'T BOTH GET WHAT WE WANT.
HOW?
WE WORK TOGETHER, BRING THE PIECE BACK TO GOTHAM. THEN WE'RE THE ONES IN POWER. THEY NEED US AND WE DECIDE WHO TO WORK WITH.
YOU WANT TO BE IN CONTROL, DON'T YOU?
TOGETHER.
"MAKES YOU WONDER WHO ELSE'S THROATS THEY'D BE WILLING TO SLIT, DOESN'T IT?"
CATWOMAN SAID IT SHOULD BE RIGHT THROUGH HERE.
THE INSCRIPTION TELLS US HOW TO OPEN THE DOOR BUT IT'S FADED.
DOESN'T MATTER. RIDDLER TOLD ME EVERYTHING I NEED TO KNOW ABOUT IT.

TOO HEAVY.
"LIFE IS BLOOD, SHED AND OFFERED. THE EAGLE'S EYE CAN FACE THIS DREE. TO BEASTS OF CHASE THE LIE IS PROFFERED: **TIMOR MORTIS CONTURBAT ME.**"
WHAT DOES IT MEAN?
"THE FEAR OF DEATH DISTURBS ME."
THE DOOR OPENS WHEN YOU GIVE IT **BLOOD,** KIRK.
BLAM
A PLEASURE WORKING WITH YOU.

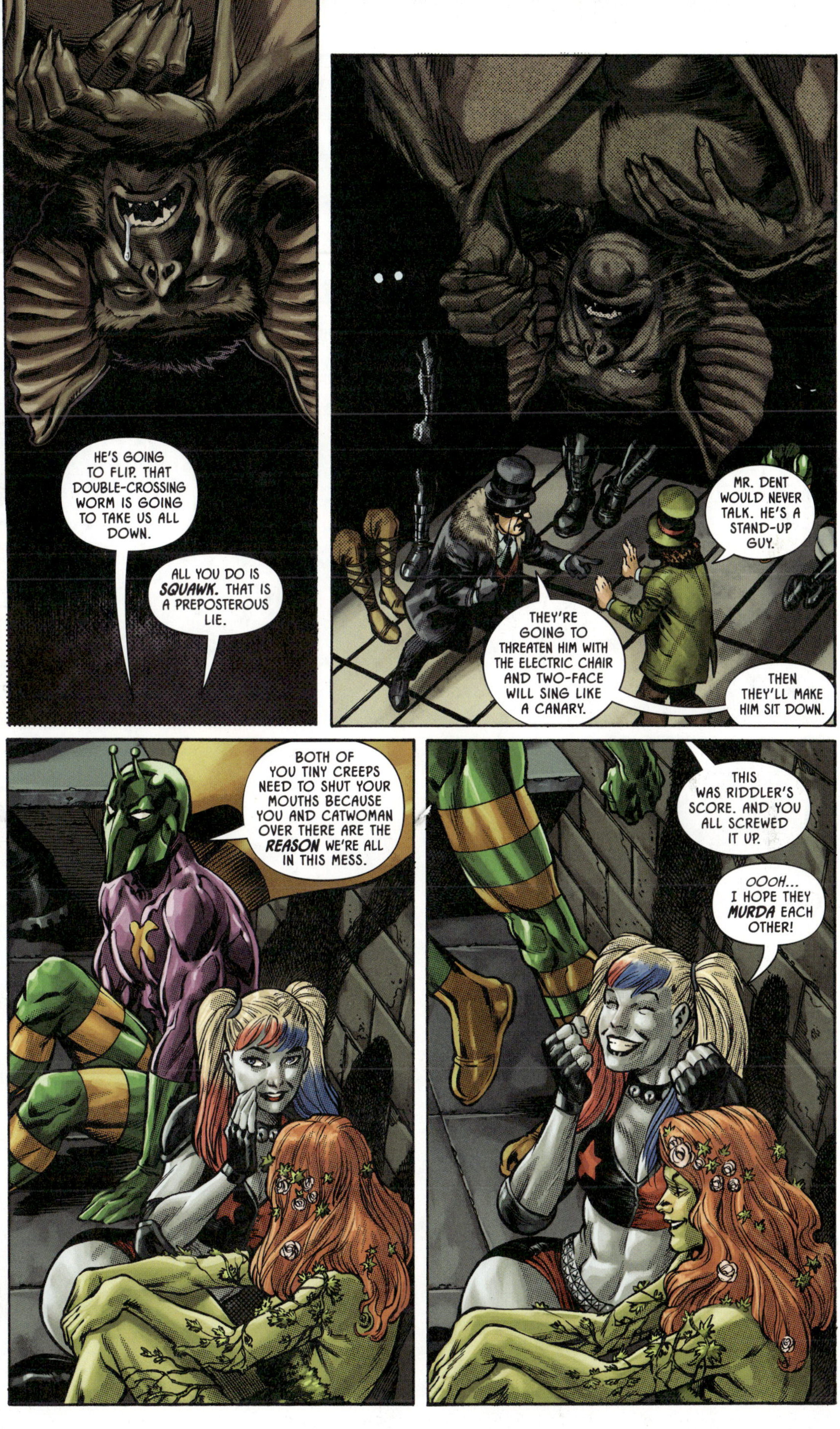
HE'S GOING TO FLIP. THAT DOUBLE-CROSSING WORM IS GOING TO TAKE US ALL DOWN.
ALL YOU DO IS SQUAWK. THAT IS A PREPOSTEROUS LIE.
MR. DENT WOULD NEVER TALK. HE'S A STAND-UP GUY.
THEY'RE GOING TO THREATEN HIM WITH THE ELECTRIC CHAIR AND TWO-FACE WILL SING LIKE A CANARY.
THEN THEY'LL MAKE HIM SIT DOWN.
BOTH OF YOU TINY CREEPS NEED TO SHUT YOUR MOUTHS BECAUSE YOU AND CATWOMAN OVER THERE ARE THE REASON WE'RE ALL IN THIS MESS.
THIS WAS RIDDLER'S SCORE. AND YOU ALL SCREWED IT UP.
OOOH... I HOPE THEY MURDA EACH OTHER!

LIKE YOU WOULDN'T HAVE DONE THE SAME.
MIND YOUR BUSINESS, SCARECROW. REMEMBER YOU AIN'T SO SCARY WITHOUT YOUR GAS.
ARE YOU SURE?
I'M NOT AFRAID OF YOU.
WHY NOT, MOTH MAN?
MAYBE YOU DIDN'T HEAR? I WENT ONE-ON-ONE WITH THE MAN-BAT. AND I PUT HIM DOWN.
OH, REALLY?
SSS...
THAT MAN-BAT?
YEAH. UMM... I GUESS BATS HEAL FAST OR SOMETHING... BECAUSE I KILLED HIM... BASICALLY.
IF I'D TRIED TO KILL THE MAN-BAT AND FAILED, I'D BE TRYING TO MAKE ALL THE FRIENDS I COULD RIGHT NOW, MOTH.
I WILL BE HIS FRIEND.
HSSSS...
SIT DOWN, BANE. NOT YOUR FIGHT.
YOU DON'T GET TO DECIDE WHAT IS AND WHAT IS NOT MY FIGHT, CROCODILE.

RAAAHH!
BUT YOU CAN EASILY INFLUENCE MY DECISION.
COME HERE, PIGGLY WIGGLY!

WHAT DO WE DO?
LET THEM FIGHT.
IF ONE OF THEM GETS KILLED, GORDON WILL HAVE OUR BADGES.
HEY! EVERYONE CALM DOWN! DON'T MAKE US GO IN THERE!
GOOD EVENING, OFFICERS. CAN I BORROW YOUR GUNS?
EVERYONE STOP!
NOW!
WHAT ARE YOU DOING?!
I'M GOING IN. WE HAVE TO STOP THEM.
WAIT FOR BACKUP!
THE BUG GUY WILL BE DEAD BY THEN.

EVERYONE AGAINST THE WALL NOW!
AARRGH!
CRAKK!
WE'RE LEAVING NOW.
OPEN THE DOOR OR HE DIES.
LET US OUT, AL. JUST DO WHAT HE SAYS.
LET HIM GO, FREEZE! YOU WON'T MAKE IT OUT OF THE STATION.
QUIET!
YOU IMBECILE! YOU'RE RUINING--
OH MY GOD!

SHRREEEE!
THANK YOU...UMM... MAN-BAT?
TEN MINUTES LATER.
SO THAT... MAN-BAT THING SAVED WALSH'S LIFE?
THAT'S WHAT THEY SAID.
WOW...
I STILL WANT TO KILL IT.
Next: IT'S TIME TO REPORT A CRIME!

The Joker Presents: A Puzzlebox #4 cover by CHIP ZDARSKY

GCPD.
WAKE UP, SCUMBAG! WHAT DOES ANY OF THIS HAVE TO DO WITH THE RIDDLER'S MURDER?!
APOLOGIES. I GOT LOST IN THOUGHT THERE FOR A MINUTE.
SLAM!
IT'S VERY THERAPEUTIC TALKING WITH YOU. YOU HAVE A CALMING AURA.
PD
DID I TELL YOU ABOUT MY OLD DOCTOR AT ARKHAM? HE USED TO--
$#!@ THIS. I'M GONNA GO TAKE A LEAK.
HE STOLE MY HAT! I'M LOCKED IN HERE FOR NO REASON BUT NOBODY TRIES TO ARREST THE B--
YOU SHOULD TAKE HIM FOR WALKS MORE OFTEN.
CUTE.
NOW WHERE WAS I? OH, YES. THE RIDDLER'S MURDER--
WE SHOULD WAIT FOR DETECTIVE BULLOCK TO COME BACK--
NO NEED...
PD

THE JUNGLES OF TROPIDOR.
THE JOKER PRESENTS: A PUZZLEBOX
CHAPTER 7: Welcome to the Jungle
SOMETHING IS WRONG! PENGUIN, OUR SIDE WAS SET UP.
THEY KNEW TWO-FACE WAS COMING ALL ALONG. WHEN THEY FOUND MAN-BAT HE COULD BARELY GET UP.
CALM DOWN, HATTER.
MATTHEW ROSENBERG writer
JESÚS MERINO, VANESA DEL REY, RICARDO LÓPEZ ORTIZ artists
ULISES ARREOLA, EVA DE LA CRUZ, TONY AVIÑA colors
FERRAN DELGADO letterer
BATMAN created by BOB KANE with BILL FINGER
CALM DOWN? WE'RE ON THE LOSING SIDE!
THE ONLY SIDE I'M ON IS MY OWN. AND I HAVE MADE SURE I WON'T LOSE.
YOU SOUND LIKE THAT VILE CLOWN. I ALMOST DIED.
I WAS BEATEN BY HARLEY QUINN. HARLEY QUINN, OF ALL PEOPLE! I'VE NEVER FELT ANYTHING SO HUMILIATIN'. THIS--
THE RHYMING IS SOMEHOW EVEN MORE ANNOYING OVER THE PHONE. I THOUGHT YOU WERE GOING TO SPEAK WITH SOMEONE ABOUT THAT?
IT'S A NERVOUS CONDITION. BESIDES THE RHYMING BRINGS ME LUCK. I DON'T DO IT OF MY OWN VOLITION AND IF IT ANNOYS YOU I DON'T GIVE A--
WHY ARE YOU CALLING ME?
YOU'RE WALKING INTO A TRAP. I--
I AM. BUT I SET IT. WORRY ABOUT YOURSELF, TETCH. GOODBYE.
CLIC!
HANG UP ON ME? HOW DARE HE!
I DON'T NEED TO WORRY ABOUT MYSELF. I...
...OH, NO.

"I DON'T THINK THIS HAS ANYTHING MORE TO DO WITH THE RIDDLER'S DEATH THAN THE LAST FEW STORIES, JOKER."
"OH YE OF LITTLE FAITH, CHIEF GORDON. IT HAS EVERYTHING TO DO WITH IT."
DON'T BE SCARED.
I'M NOT.
YES, WE ARE. BUT WE WILL OUTWIT HIM. HE'S JUST... BIG.
HE'S NOT THAT BIG.
PAF
YES, HE IS. AND HE WILL CRUSH US INTO THE GROUND IF WE GO NEAR HIM. LEAVE NOW.
DON'T LISTEN TO YOU. YOU'RE A COWARD, OSWALD.
WOOOOSH
LEAVE NOW, OSWALD. DON'T LET OSWALD TALK YOU INTO PLAYING CATWOMAN'S GAMES.
PAKA PAKA PAKA PAKA
IF BANE COMES NEAR US, WE'LL KILL HIM.

"SO THE PENGUIN HAS VOICES IN HIS HEAD NOW, JOKER?"
"WHEN YOU LOOK AT THAT LITTLE MAN, DO YOU BELIEVE HE IS MENTALLY WELL?"
A LABYRINTH? REALLY? THIS IS ABSURD.
"THIS IS ABSURD."
SLASH
I'M GOING TO MURDER SOMEONE WHEN THIS IS ALL OVER.
"TOLD YA HE WAS OFF..."

VS
"...WITH BANE HAVING THE ADVANTAGE IN SIZE, STRENGTH, STAMINA, AND JUST ABOUT EVERY OTHER WAY WE MEASURE A PERSON...
"...IT WAS UP TO OSWALD TO RELY ON HIS *WITS* TO BEAT HIM THROUGH THIS LABYRITH.
SMASH
"POOR OSWALD."
EXIT

I KNEW I COULD BEAT THAT STEROID-FUELED MONSTER.
HELLO. WOULD YOU LIKE TO PLAY A GAME?
TWEEDLE-DEE AND TWEEDLEDUM?! WHAT THE HELL IS THIS NOW?
THE RIDDLER TRUSTED US TO GUARD THE PATH. HE WAS WORRIED SOMEONE WAS TRYING TO STEAL HIS THINGS.
WHY NOT JUST HAVE YOU BRING THEM TO HIM?
HE DOESN'T TRUST US ENOUGH FOR THAT. WE SIMPLY GUARD THE PATHS AND RECITE THE RIDDLE.
TWO PATHS. ONE LEADS TO WHAT YOU SEEK. ONE LEADS TO CERTAIN DOOM.
ALWAYS ANOTHER GAME WITH THIS IDIOT... PATHS PLURAL?
SIGH WHICH IS WHICH?
WE'RE AFRAID WE CANNOT SAY.
WE DO KNOW.
IF YOU DON'T KNOW, THEN WHY ARE YOU HERE?
THEN TELL ME.
YOU CAN ASK ONE QUESTION OF ONE OF US. BUT BEWARE, ONE OF US WILL ALWAYS LIE TO YOU, AND ONE WILL ALWAYS TELL THE TRUTH. BUT WE CAN'T TELL YOU WHICH IS WHICH.
I'VE MET YOU BEFORE. YOU BOTH LIE A LOT.
WOULD YOU LIKE TO PLAY?

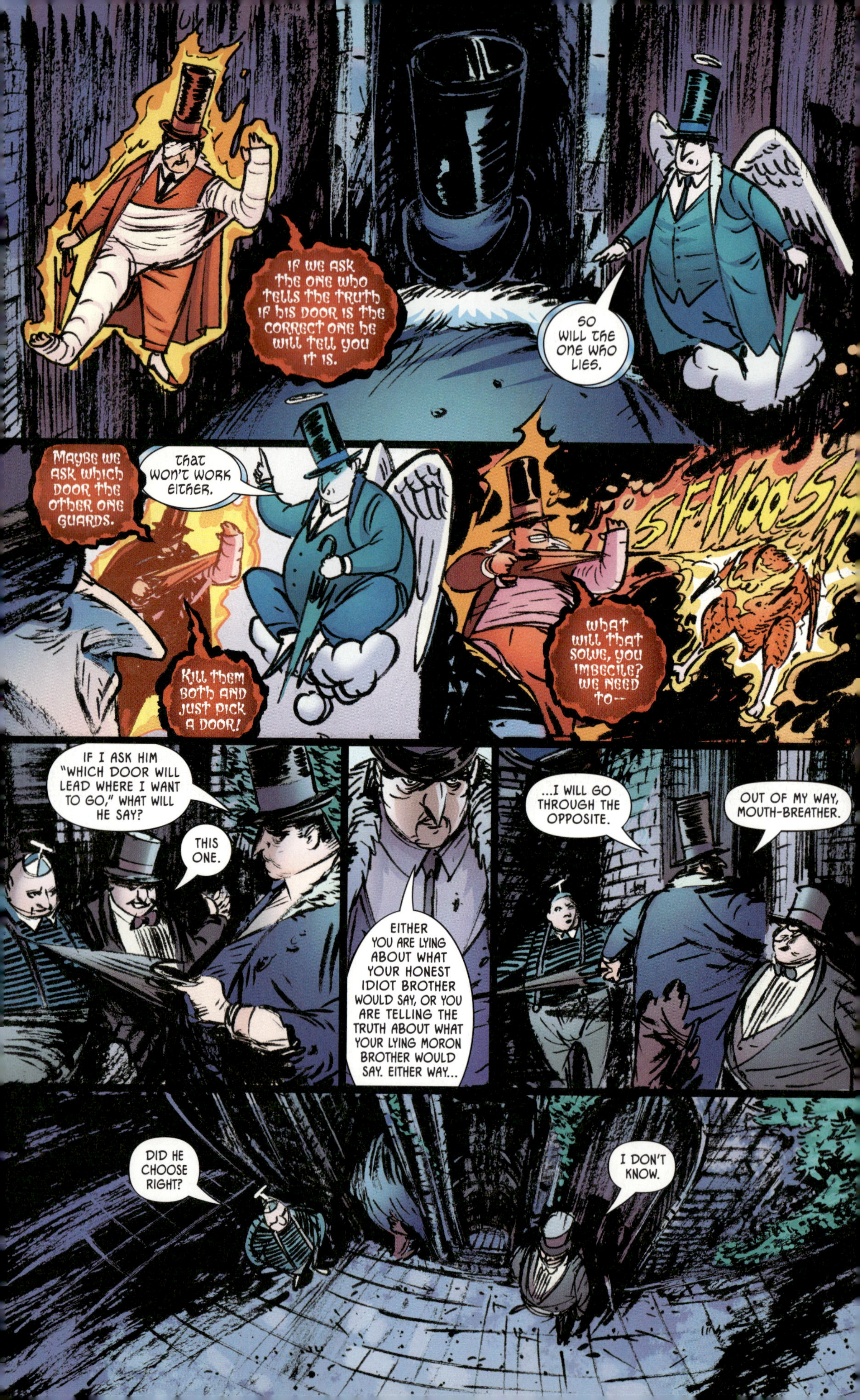
IF WE ASK THE ONE WHO TELLS THE TRUTH IF HIS DOOR IS THE CORRECT ONE HE WILL TELL YOU IT IS.
SO WILL THE ONE WHO LIES.
MAYBE WE ASK WHICH DOOR THE OTHER ONE GUARDS.
THAT WON'T WORK EITHER.
SFWOOSH
WHAT WILL THAT SOWE, YOU IMBECILE? WE NEED TO--
KILL THEM BOTH AND JUST PICK A DOOR!
IF I ASK HIM "WHICH DOOR WILL LEAD WHERE I WANT TO GO," WHAT WILL HE SAY?
THIS ONE.
EITHER YOU ARE LYING ABOUT WHAT YOUR HONEST IDIOT BROTHER WOULD SAY, OR YOU ARE TELLING THE TRUTH ABOUT WHAT YOUR LYING MORON BROTHER WOULD SAY. EITHER WAY...
...I WILL GO THROUGH THE OPPOSITE.
OUT OF MY WAY, MOUTH-BREATHER.
DID HE CHOOSE RIGHT?
I DON'T KNOW.

"HOW COULD YOU POSSIBLY KNOW HE SAID THAT IF YOU WEREN'T THERE?"
I HATE RIDDLES.
"IT JUST SEEMS LIKELY. MOST PEOPLE DO."
HELLO. WOULD YOU LIKE TO PLAY A GAME?
WHICH WAY DID THE PENGUIN GO?
I TOLD YOU WE COULD BEAT HIM HERE WITHOUT CHEATING.
THAT'S NOT HOW IT WORKS.
That ape will never be able to solve it. Maybe he'll die.
POW
WHAM
KRACK
OWW!
OH %&!*.
THAT WAY! HE WENT THROUGH THAT DOOR!
CRASH

YOU'RE TOO LATE, BANE. ONCE AGAIN BEING A SHAVED GORILLA IN A MEXICAN WRESTLING MASK HAS NOT PROVED TO BE AN ADVANTAGE WHEN FACING A SUPERIOR INTELLECT.
I GOT HERE FIRST.
WHY WOULD I CARE WHO GOT HERE FIRST?
THAT IS... VALID. THEN I GUESS YOU WISH TO FIGHT ME?
BANG
BANG
SO BE IT, BEHEMOTH.
CRACK
YOU'RE MAKING A TREMENDOUS--
--MISTAAAKE!
THUMP
STUPID MAN.
"STUPIDITY IS BRIEF AND ARTLESS, WHILE INTELLIGENCE SQUIRMS AND HIDES ITSELF. INTELLIGENCE IS UNPRINCIPLED, BUT STUPIDITY IS HONEST AND STRAIGHTFORWARD."

THAT FELT A BIT UNCALLED FOR.
I THOUGHT SO. AND WHAT WAS THAT NONSENSE HE BABBLED ON HIS WAY OUT? TRYING TO SOUND SMART.
HE WAS QUOTING DOSTOYEVSKY. BUT I'M SURE YOU KNOW THAT, BEING SUCH AN INTELLECTUAL AND ALL.
YOU PAID ME TO TRICK HIM, NOT FIGHT HIM, OSWALD.
OF COURSE I DID. AND THANK YOU FOR THE HELP THERE.
SPEAKING OF...
HERE IS YOUR PRECIOUS ARTIFACT.
I WAS ABLE TO SNEAK THROUGH THE VINES AND GET PAST THE RIDDLER'S LITTLE HELPERS WITH EASE, JUST LIKE YOU SUGGESTED.
NOW WHAT, MAY I ASK, IS IT?
I PAID YOU **GENEROUSLY** TO PLACE A REPLICA, NOT ASK QUESTIONS, ***PAMELA...***
SO MIND YOUR BUSINESS.
TURNS OUT BRAIN BEATS BRAWN AFTER ALL.
LUCKY FOR ME I HAVE BOTH.

GCPD.
SO YOU NEVER GOT INTO TOLKIEN?
HE'S FINE.
ALICE IN WONDERLAND IS OKAY, I GUESS. BUT LORD OF THE RINGS IS MY FAVORITE.
NOT MINE.
I MEAN, I HAVEN'T READ THE BOOKS YET. BUT THE MOVIES ARE GREAT. YOU SHOULD CHECK THEM OUT--
NO!
DON'T LET HIM HIT ME!
WHUMP!

DO NOT MOVE, SIONIS!
I DIDN'T @#%$?&* DO ANYTHING!
MY CLIENT IS COMPLYING!
THUMP!!
GET HIM OUTTA HERE!
I'LL SEE YOU LATER, LITTLE MAN.
THEY'RE ALL TRYING TO GET ME, YOU SEE? THEY PICK ON ME FOR MY SIZE.
I APOLOGIZE. SORRY ABOUT THAT.
IT'S FINE. YOU OKAY?
LET ME GET YOU YOUR HAT.
I'M SURE THEY JUST DO IT FOR A LAUGH.
IT'S SO...
...OOH...
VERY NICE HAT. SIZE SEVEN AND ONE HALF?
YEAH... I GUESS.

PRISONER JERVIS TETCH. YOU ALL NEED ANYTHING ELSE?
NO, I THINK THAT'LL BE ALL. THANKS.
WHY DON'T YOU HAVE A SEAT, MR. TETCH.
NO, THAT WILL NOT BE ALL. YOU SHOULD HAVE PAID ME MORE ATTENTION WHEN WE WERE IN THE HALL.
NOW YOU MUST FOLLOW MY WORD AS IF IT WERE YOUR OATH!
I COMMAND YOU TO KILL THEM BOTH!

UMM... WHAT?
WHO ARE YOU TALKING TO?
YOU! I AM COMMANDING YOU!
WHATEVER I SAY, YOU MUST DO, OFFICER...
I CAN'T READ IT FROM HERE... IS IT OFFICER... BANDERSNATCH?
6
UMM...IT'S ANDERSON.
ANDERSON
WHO CARES.
I COMMAND YOU, OFFICER ANDERSON, TO SHOOT THEM AND ESCORT ME FROM THIS JAIL WHILE YOUR FELLOWS ARE STILL UNAWARE!
...NO?

YOU SURE YOU DON'T NEED ANYTHING ELSE?
WE'RE ALL GOOD HERE, OFFICER ANDERSON.
YEAH, THAT'S GOOD. TAKE A SEAT, MR. TETCH.
WE WANTED TO ASK YOU SOME QUESTIONS ABOUT THE MURDER OF THE RIDDLER.
HE ROBBED ME!
THE RIDDLER? THAT MUST HAVE MADE YOU VERY--
NOT THE RIDDLER. HE WAS AS NICE AS CAN BE.
I'M CONFUSED. WHO ROBBED YOU? OFFICER BANDERSNATCH?
IF SHE TOOK ANYTHING WE CAN HELP YOU FILL OUT A REPORT AFTER YOU ANSWER A FEW QUESTIONS--
IT WAS THE BAT!
THE AWFUL MAN, HE STOLE MY HAT!
YOU'RE WEARING YOUR HAT RIGHT NOW.
I KNOW WHAT WAS DONE. DON'T YOU THINK I OWN MORE THAN ONE HAT, YOU DISGUSTING SIMPLETON?
OF COURSE YOU DO. WHO DOESN'T OWN A FEW HATS THE SIZE OF THEIR OWN BODY?

HERE'S WHAT YOU SHOULD KNOW.
HE TOOK IT A FEW DAYS AGO.
WHY DIDN'T YOU REPORT IT THEN? CASE LIKE THIS, LEADS GROW COLD.
HE MIGHT NOT HAVE WANTED TO BECAUSE HE IS A WANTED FELON. AND IT DIDN'T HAPPEN.
OH, YEAH. THERE'S THAT.
I HAVE NO CLUE!
I WAS TRYING TO USE MY HAT TO MIND CONTROL... WHATSHERFACE INTO MURDERING BOTH OF YOU...
YEAH, WE PICKED UP ON THAT.
...WAIT!
YOU WANTED HELP FROM ME? I KNOW WHAT HAPPENED!
WITH THE RIDDLER?
THE BAT MUST BE USING MY TECHNOLOGY.
GUESS NOT.
HE WANTS OTHERS TO BE ENTRAPPENED.
IS THAT A WORD?
MY HAT DIDN'T WORK NOW DUE TO INTERFERENCE. IT'S SOMEWHERE NEARBY.
THAT EXPLAINS ITS ORIGINAL DISAPPEARANCE.
YOU THINK BATMAN IS IN THIS BUILDING, RIGHT NOW, WEARING YOUR HAT?
SO BATMAN STOLE YOUR HAT, BUT THEN HID IT IN A POLICE PRECINCT?
MAYBE THE BAT IS HERE, MAYBE NOT. BUT MY HAT IS HERE, EVEN IF HE ISN'T CAUGHT.
DON'T BE SO DENSE. IT'S THE ONLY EXPLANATION THAT MAKES ANY SENSE.
PLOC!
THIS CLEARLY ISN'T GOING TO GET US ANYTHING GOOD. WANT TO GRAB SOME BREAKFAST, MONTOYA?

WRAMM!
IF I DIDN'T KNOW BETTER, OFFICER BULLOCK, I'D SAY YOU DON'T REALLY LIKE ME.
WASTING OUR DAMN TIME LIKE IT'S A GAME. I'M--
HARVEY! THAT'S ENOUGH. WHY DON'T YOU TAKE A WALK?
BYE-BYE, HARV. NICE CHATTING WITH YOU.
I APOLOGIZE. WE'RE ALL A LITTLE TIRED AND ON EDGE HERE, BUT THAT'S NO EXCUSE.
ANY LUCK FINDING ME THAT DONUT?
I...I FORGOT.
POLICE MISCONDUCT TAKES MANY SHAPES, DOESN'T IT?
ALAS, WE SHOULD PROBABLY DISCUSS THE MUSEUM. IT'S WHY WE'RE HERE, AFTER ALL.

GATEWAY CITY.
AN EPIC EXHIBIT FOR OUR TIMES–
BEHOLD THE NEW GODS
"YOU'RE REFERRING TO THE COLLETTA HISTORY MUSEUM INCIDENT, JOKER?"
"I CAN SEE WHY THEY MADE YOU THE PRESIDENT OF DETECTIVES, JIM."
"YOU'RE TELLING ME THIS WAS RELATED TO THE RIDDLER'S MURDER?"
"DON'T YOU SEE YET? IT'S ALL RELATED.
CRASH!!
"EVERYONE KNOWS THAT PROFESSOR PYG QUIETLY SNUCK INTO THE MUSEUM THAT NIGHT.
"BUT WHAT YOU COULDN'T POSSIBLY KNOW IS THAT SOMEONE ELSE FOLLOWED HIM..."
"YEAH, SCARECROW. HE SPOKE TO A FEW GUARDS AND WAS CAUGHT ON THE SECURITY CAMERAS."
"OH...HMM... I GUESS YOU COULD POSSIBLY KNOW."

"THEN I'M SURE YOU ALSO KNOW THAT THE MUSEUM HOUSED THE FINAL PIECE OF THE MASTER ENGINE."
HELP... ME...
NO.
"EVEN IF THEY DIDN'T KNOW WHAT IT WAS."
HE'S KILLING THEM!
CALL 9-1-1. TELL THEM TO GET EVERYONE DOWN HERE RIGHT--
I'M AFRAID I CAN'T LET YOU DO THAT.
FRSSH!
CALM YOUR PRETTY LITTLE HEAD. I'M JUST HERE TO WATCH THE SHOW.
FRSSH!!
PLEASE, NO!

I'M IN THE MUSEUM.
I'M NOT GIVING OUT PRIZES FOR ALMOST DOING THE JOB, SCARECROW.
THE SECURITY SYSTEMS HERE ARE... ELABORATE. SO I'VE DECIDED TO WAIT.
WAIT FOR WHAT EXACTLY?
SOMEONE IS HANDLING IT FOR ME.
DO YOU MEAN PROFESSOR PYG?
YES.
ARE YOU OUT OF YOUR DAMN MIND, CRANE?
IF YOU WANTED SOMEONE WHO COULD BYPASS THE SECURITY SYSTEMS, PERHAPS YOU SHOULD HAVE COME DOWN AND DONE THE JOB YOURSELF, CATWOMAN.
I AM INDISPOSED.
I'M SURE. BUT IF I TRIED TO DO IT, I'D SET OFF THE ALARMS AND THE POLICE WOULD BE ALL OVER ME BEFORE I STEPPED OUT THE DOOR.
AND WHAT, MY DEAR SCARECROW, DO YOU THINK PYG IS GOING TO DO?
AWOOAWOO
IF YOU'LL EXCUSE ME, I HAVE TO GO NOW.

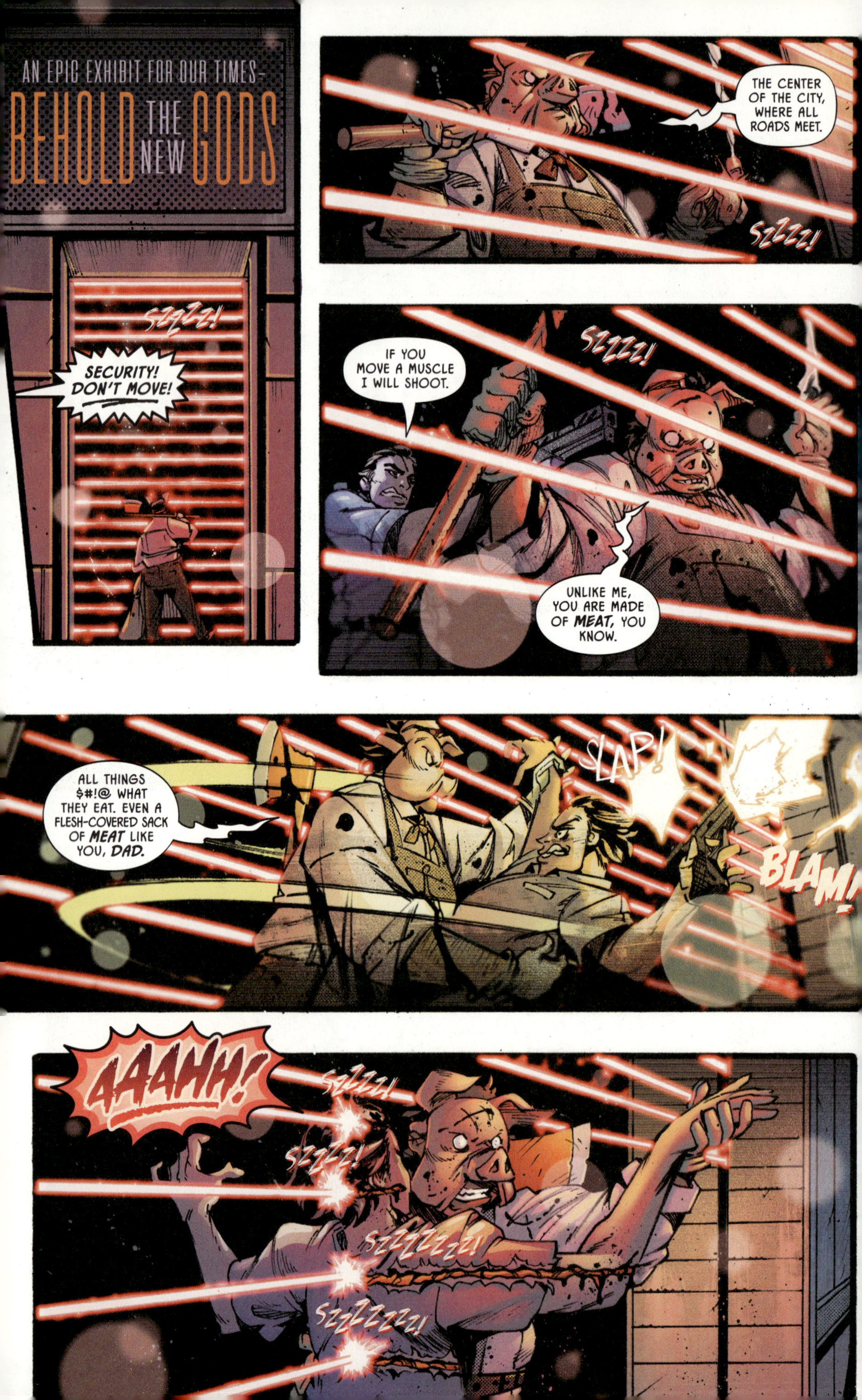
AN EPIC EXHIBIT FOR OUR TIMES–
BEHOLD THE NEW GODS
SZZZZ!
SECURITY! DON'T MOVE!
THE CENTER OF THE CITY, WHERE ALL ROADS MEET.
SZZZZ!
SZZZZ!
IF YOU MOVE A MUSCLE I WILL SHOOT.
UNLIKE ME, YOU ARE MADE OF MEAT, YOU KNOW.
ALL THINGS $#!@ WHAT THEY EAT. EVEN A FLESH-COVERED SACK OF MEAT LIKE YOU, DAD.
SLAP!
BLAM!
AAAHH!
SZZZZ!
SZZZZ!
SZZZZZZZZ!
SZZZZZZZZ!

GOOD GOD.
AN EPIC EXHIBIT FOR OUR TIMES—
BEHOLD THE NEW GODS
OFF TO WORK WE GO.
I BELIEVE YOU HAVE SOMETHING I NEED, PROFESSOR.
JUST ONE?
DROP THE BAG AND YOU CAN GO.
I'LL DROP MY *OH*-SO-LITTLE BAG...
THUD!
...BUT I DON'T KNOW THAT I'LL *GO*.

FRSSH!
Sniff! Sniff!
VERY SCARY.
THAT'S NOT POSSIBLE...
IT'S PROBABLE!

"DOES THIS EXPLAIN WHY ONE OF THESE MEN KILLED THE RIDDLER?"
"YOU NEED TO LOOK AT THE SUBTEXT HERE, JIM."
"WHY DON'T YOU HELP ME OUT AND MAKE IT THE TEXT?"
WHUMP!
I'LL KILL YOU AND THEN I'LL KILL THE RIDDLER!
"THAT'S NOT WHAT I MEANT."
NOT IF I KILL HIM FIRST!
CRASH!
WEOOWEOOWEOO
OOOF.

LET IT GO, YOU FOOL.
NO.
GATEWAY POLICE! DROP YOUR WEAPONS!
FINE. I WON'T BE CAUGHT BECAUSE OF YOU.
HELLO, OFFICERS OF THE LAW. THANKS FOR COMING TO MY PARTY.
IT'S ME AGAIN. THE POLICE ARE HERE. I NEED YOUR HELP.
DID YOU GET THE ARTIFACT?
NO. PYG HAS IT STILL.
CAN YOU GET IT BACK FROM HIM?
NO. HE'S PROBABLY FIGHTING HALF THE GATEWAY POLICE DEPARTMENT NOW.
THEN WHAT DO YOU EXPECT ME TO DO FOR YOU, SCARECROW?
AN EPIC EXHIBIT FOR OUR T
I HIRED YOU FOR A JOB AND YOU--
PARDON?
SHUT UP.
IT'S YOUR LUCKY DAY, SELINA.

I'VE GOT YOUR LITTLE PIECE OF THE BOX. BE THANKFUL YOU DIDN'T HIRE A CRAZY PERSON TO DO THIS.
NO, I HIRED A MORON WHO--
CLICK!
BOOM!
EVERYBODY WANTS TO LOOK AT PYG'S TREASURE!
LINE UP TO SEE WHAT I STOLE!

GCPD.
EVERYTHING I DID WAS ON PURPOSE.
I SHOT HIM IN HIS WIDOW'S PEAK. IF I AM LOCKED IN HERE, I LOCKED MYSELF IN THIS CAGE TO PROTECT MYSELF FROM WHAT IS COMING FOR MYSELF.
BUT THE TIME IS COMING FOR PYGS TO FLY.
TAKE FLIGHT INTO THE NIGHT AND BECOME FREE FROM THIS BOX OF MY OWN MAKING.
I HAVE AN IDEA.
OH, PROFESSOR. MAY I HAVE A WORD?

NOBODY TELLS PYG WHAT TO DO!
I'LL SKIN A CAT FOR THAT.
KRAKK!
AGK!
THAT'S ENOUGH.
LET IT PLAY OUT, APE.
GASP
GUARDS! GET HIM OFF ME!

GET OFF HER, PYG!
EVERYONE BACK AGAINST THE WALL!
I SAID OFF!
BZZZZT!
SQUEEEEE!
YOU'RE COMING WITH US.
WHAT THE HELL IS THIS?
WE GOTTA PUT HIM IN THE SOLITARY HOLDING CELL. HE WAS TRYING TO EAT THE CAT LADY.
NO @#$&. AND YOU STOPPED HIM?

I WASN'T TRYING TO EAT HER...
...DON'T LIE ABOUT ME!
HE'S GOT A GUN!
GET DOWN!
KA-BLAM!
NOW THE FOOT IS ON THE OTHER SHOE!
LOOK OUT!
YES, LOOK AT ME! LOOK AT ME!
MORONS.
CCPD

EMERGENCY EXIT
SOMEONE STOP HIM!
GET SOME MEN DOWN ON THE STREET TO CUT HIM OFF!
ROOF
STREET
RAIN?
STRANGE. I THOUGHT IT WAS GOING TO BE SUNNY WHEN I GOT OUT.
STAIRS
SO THAT'S HOW THEY CALL HIM.
KA-THUNK!
OOOH. IT'S BRIGHT.

PUT IT DOWN, PYG!
NO. I DON'T THINK SO.
PUT IT DOWN AND WE CAN TALK.
WHY WOULD YOU THINK I WANT TO HEAR ANYTHING EVER COME OUT OF YOUR MOUTH? YOU ARE A--
WHUMP!
OW!
THANK YOU, BATMAN.
I WAS IN THE AREA WHEN I SAW THE SIGNAL. DON'T LET HIM ESCAPE AGAIN.
NONE OF YOU UNDERSTAND. THE JOKER DIDN'T KILL HIM. *I DID!*
I KILLED THE RIDDLER AS MUCH AS HE DID. AND THE BOX IS *FAKE.* AND THE BATMAN IS *FAKE.*
Next Issue:
THE CAT IS OUT OF THE BOX!

The Joker Presents: A Puzzlebox #5 cover by CHIP ZDARSKY

LOOK WHO'S BACK. WHAT'S THE MATTER, HARV? NO MORE EVIDENCE TO PLANT THIS EVENING?
GCPD.
I BROUGHT YOU THAT DONUT YOU'VE BEEN ASKING FOR ALL NIGHT.
DO YOU REALLY THINK I'LL FORGET YOU ASSAULTED ME EARLIER IF YOU GIVE ME BAKED GOODS?
BECAUSE I TOTALLY WILL!
Sniff Sniff
SMELLS WEIRD.
NOW WHERE WAS I? OH, RIGHT. YOUR LITTLE MURDER.

THE JOKER PRESENTS: A PUZZLEBOX
CHAPTER 9:
The more things come together...
MATTHEW ROSENBERG writer
JESÚS MERINO, CHRIS MOONEYHAM, FREDDIE E. WILLIAMS II artists
ULISES ARREOLA, ROMAN STEVENS colors
FERRAN DELGADO letterer
"THESE THINGS BEGAN LIKE THEY ALWAYS DO. ANOTHER OF GOTHAM'S *MENTALLY UNWELL CITIZENS* OUT FOR A STROLL."
BATMAN created by BOB KANE with BILL FINGER.
SUPERMAN created by JERRY SIEGEL and JOE SHUSTER.
By Special Arrangement with the JERRY SIEGEL FAMILY.
SPARE SOME CHANGE TO BUY ME A TICKET OUTTA THIS TOWN?
LADY, IF TONIGHT DOESN'T GO RIGHT I'LL NEED WHAT I GOT FOR *MY OWN* BUS TICKET OUT.
EASY NOW, DRURY. IT'S NOT A TRAP...
PROBABLY.

CLICK
SHOULD HAVE LISTENED TO YOUR GUT, MOTH. IT'S DEFINITELY A TRAP.
TWO-FACE? YOU SURE YOU REALLY WANT TO GO ALONE AGAINST THE RIDDLER AND HIS PEOPLE?
I THOUGHT MOTHS COULD SEE IN THE DARK...
I'M NOT ALONE.
HELLO, MOTH. HOPE YOU AND THE RIDDLER DON'T MIND THAT I INVITED SOME FRIENDS.
CATWOMAN. I DON'T THINK YOU WERE INVITED.
GIRL LIKE ME CAN'T SIT AROUND WAITING FOR INVITATIONS, NOW CAN I?
AND BESIDES, SOME OF MY FRIENDS WERE DYING TO SEE YOU AGAIN. ISN'T THAT RIGHT, MAN-BAT?
OH, HEY... MAN...BAT. UMM... SORRY ABOUT ALL THAT. GLAD TO SEE YOU'RE NOT DEAD.
GRRRRRRR...

YOU KNOW THAT PIECE DOESN'T DO ANYTHING ON ITS OWN.
YOU NEED ***ALL*** OF THEM. YOU THINK THE RIDDLER IS GOING TO JUST TURN THE REST OVER TO YOU?
I CAN BE PRETTY ***PERSUASIVE.***
HAHA!
THE PESKY PUSSYCAT THINKS SHE CAN BE PRETTY PERSUASIVE? SO CUTE.
IF YA WANNA PERSUADE ME YOU SHOULDA BROUGHT MORE BOYS, PUSSYCAT.
WE'RE NOT HERE TO DEAL WITH YOU, PIGTAILS. WE WERE HOPING TO TALK TO THE LITTLE MAN IN CHARGE OF THE SHOW.
THAT'S TOO BAD. BECAUSE WE ***DEFINITELY*** WANTED TO TALK TA YOU ALL TO GET BACK ALL THE PIECES OF OUR LITTLE BOX YOU STOLE.
THIS DOESN'T HAVE TO BE MESSY, HARLEY.
DOESN'T IT?

WE'RE ON THE SAME SIDE, ROID-RAGE!
WHO INVITED THEM?!
I ASSUMED YOU DID!
MOVE, APE!
WAIT! WHERE DID YOU GET A PIECE OF THE BOX, IVY?!
"AS YOU CAN SEE, THEY ARE ALL A BUNCH OF DANGEROUS DEGENERATES. FRANKLY, I'M RELIEVED YOU LOCKED THEM UP HERE."

WE DIDN'T COME LOOKING FOR A FIGHT HERE, PIGTAILS. WE JUST WANT OUR FAIR SHARE.
OF WHAT?
OF... WHATEVER IT IS THE BOX ACTUALLY DOES.
AGK!
KRAK
HA! HA! YOU DON'T EVEN KNOW WHAT IT DOES, PUSSYCAT.
DO YOU, CLOWN GIRL?
OVERGROWN MONSTER.
NO, NOT YOU! WAIT!
PSSSSSHHHHHH
EVERYBODY SHUT UP!

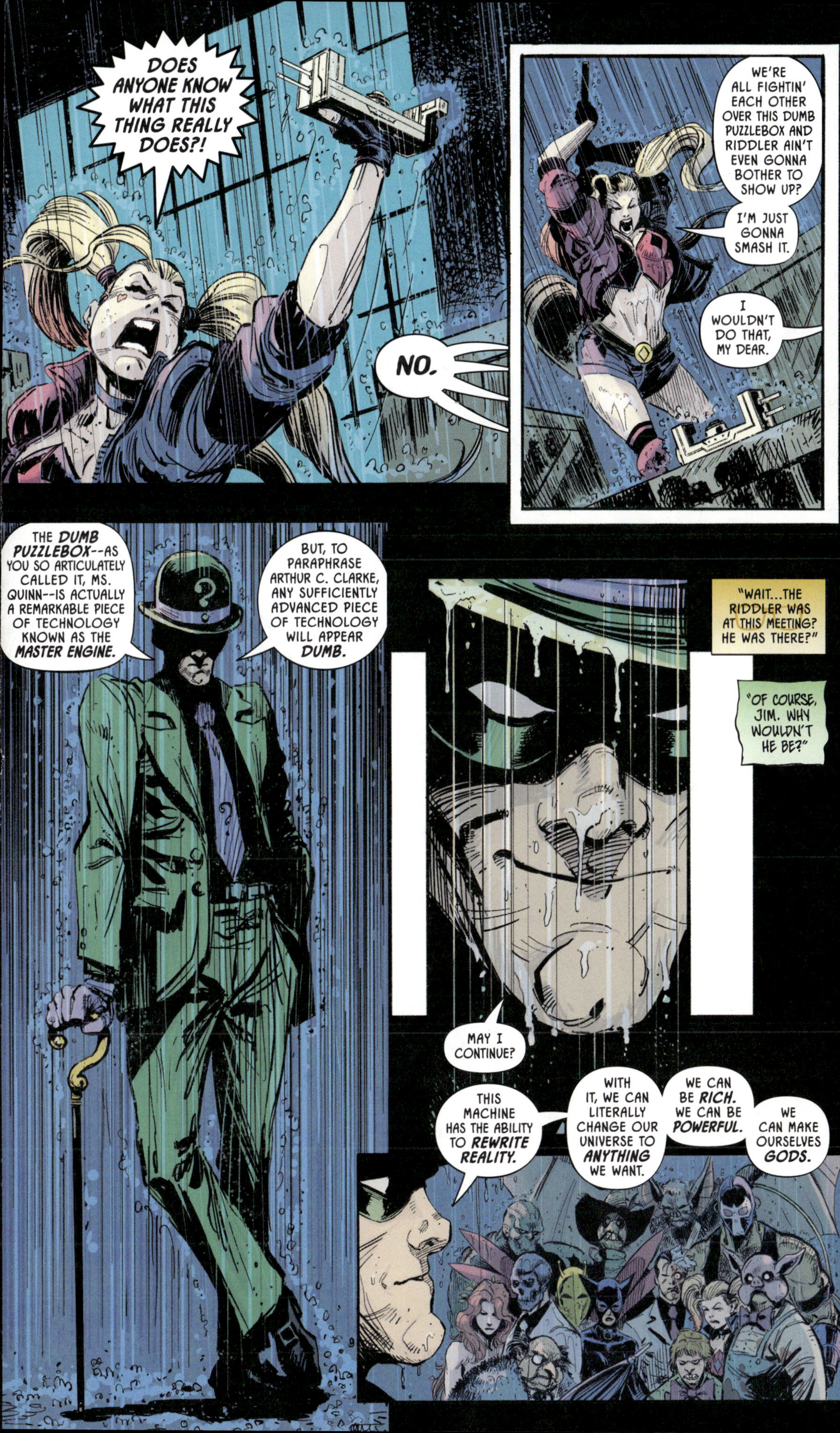

DOES ANYONE KNOW WHAT THIS THING REALLY DOES?!
NO.
WE'RE ALL FIGHTIN' EACH OTHER OVER THIS DUMB PUZZLEBOX AND RIDDLER AIN'T EVEN GONNA BOTHER TO SHOW UP?
I'M JUST GONNA SMASH IT.
I WOULDN'T DO THAT, MY DEAR.
THE DUMB PUZZLEBOX--AS YOU SO ARTICULATELY CALLED IT, MS. QUINN--IS ACTUALLY A REMARKABLE PIECE OF TECHNOLOGY KNOWN AS THE MASTER ENGINE.
BUT, TO PARAPHRASE ARTHUR C. CLARKE, ANY SUFFICIENTLY ADVANCED PIECE OF TECHNOLOGY WILL APPEAR DUMB.
"WAIT...THE RIDDLER WAS AT THIS MEETING? HE WAS THERE?"
"OF COURSE, JIM. WHY WOULDN'T HE BE?"
MAY I CONTINUE?
THIS MACHINE HAS THE ABILITY TO REWRITE REALITY.
WITH IT, WE CAN LITERALLY CHANGE OUR UNIVERSE TO ANYTHING WE WANT.
WE CAN BE RICH. WE CAN BE POWERFUL.
WE CAN MAKE OURSELVES GODS.

AND WHO DECIDES--?
WE ALL DO. I DON'T MIND THAT YOU AND YOUR PEOPLE WORKED AGAINST ME, SELINA. IT DOESN'T MATTER.
THAT'S THE NICE THING ABOUT UNLIMITED POWER. WE CAN ALL GET WHATEVER WE WANT.
THESE PETTY DISPUTES ARE BENEATH ME AND SOON THEY CAN BE BENEATH US ALL.
EVERY PERSON WHO HAS A PIECE CAN BRING IT FORWARD...
AND THEN WE CAN ALL TAKE TURNS MAKING OUR WISH...
JUST ONE?
I AM AFRAID THE DEVICE ONLY GRANTS ONE WISH. PER PERSON, OF COURSE.
THAT ONE WAS MINE!
SHUT UP, MOTH MAN.
IT'S NOT WORKING.
THAT'S BECAUSE YOURS IS FAKE. IVY TRICKED YOU...
SHE TRICKED US BOTH. ISN'T THAT RIGHT, IVY?
INDEED, IT IS, OSWALD.
BEHOLD! THE MASTER ENGINE!
IS IT SUPPOSED TO BE DOING THAT?
AHHH!
GET DOWN!

KRESSH
BLAM!
AARGH! SOMEONE IS PLAYING GAMES!
YAIEEEE!
OH, WHAT A FRIGHTFUL AFFAIR. SEEMS SOME POOR WOMAN IS SCREAMING BLOODY MURDER OUT THERE.
HEY! WHERE THE HELL DID THE RIDDLER GO?

AND WHERE'S THE DAMNED BOX?!
CHRIS MOONEYHAM

GCPD.
OFFICER, I'M NOT FEELING SO GOOD.
TOO BAD, LADY.
I JUST GOT ASSAULTED BY A LUNATIC. ON YOUR WATCH.
DON'T YOU THINK YOU SHOULD LET A PARAMEDIC CHECK ME OUT?
WHAT WOULD HAPPEN IF HAVE A BRAIN HEMORRHAGE AND DIE IN HERE BECAUSE YOU DENIED ME MEDICAL ATTENTION?
WOULD YOU GET IN TROUBLE FOR THAT?
FINE. BUT NO FUNNY BUSINESS.
I'M OFFENDED AT THE MERE SUGGESTION.

I BET YOU BOYS NEVER BEEN AROUND SO MANY PEOPLE LIKE THIS BEFORE, HUH? SOME REAL AMAZING ABILITIES IN THAT CELL.
STOP TALKING.
YOU MIGHT NOT KNOW IT FROM LOOKING AT ME, BUT I CAN DO SOME AMAZING THINGS MYSELF. I'D LOVE TO SHOW BOTH--
HE'S GOT A GUN!
KA-BLAM!
OH. THAT'LL DO NICELY.
YOU GO CHECK IT OUT. I'LL STAY WITH HER.
JUST GO!
BUT I--
DON'T SHOOT ANYONE, DAVIS!
I COULDN'T GET HIM. INITIATE PLAN B.
BACHMAN, I DON'T HAVE TIME--
JUST US NOW.
NO, I--
GOODIE. SAY, DO YOU MIND IF I GET CLEANED UP IN THE LITTLE KITTEN'S ROOM? I DON'T LIKE PEOPLE SEEING ME LIKE THIS.
I PROMISE I'M A LOT EASIER ON THE EYES THAN THIS USUALLY, HANDSOME. IT'LL BE WORTH IT.

"FINE. JUST BE QUICK."
"OFFICER, BEAUTY TAKES TIME.
"ALL GOOD THINGS TO THOSE WHO WAIT."
AHH. THAT'S BETTER.

ONE DEAD BODY. TWELVE SUSPECTS LOOKING FOR A DEAL. ALL I KNOW IS IT WAS NOT ME.
PSST
YOU'RE DOING GREAT WORK, JERVIS. KEEP THEM CONFUSED.
I'LL GET YOU OUT OF HERE SOON ENOUGH, BIG GUY.
HELLO? ARE YOU REAL?
HE TOLD ME NOT TO EVEN BOTHER APPLYING. I SAID TO HIM--
Flick!
WHAT WAS THAT?
PING!
POINT IS, I APPLIED. HE'S NEVER EVEN HEARD ME PLAY MY FLUTE.
I'M NOT FILLING THIS OUT. I'M DONE FOR THE DAY.
SECURE AREA. NO ADMITTANCE.
IF SARGE WANTS THIS REPORT TONIGHT HE CAN KISS MY !$#.
FINE, I'LL DO IT.

STUPID BACHMAN.
THIS IS SO *GROSS.*
HERE GOES NOTHING--
CLICK!
YOU NEED TO ASK FOR MORE MONEY, SELINA. ALWAYS ASK FOR MORE MONEY.

HEY! IF YOU'RE NOT OUT IN THREE SECONDS I'M COMING IN, LADY!
NOK! NOK!
I DON'T CARE WHAT YOU'RE DOING--
NO NEED TO BE RUDE, OFFICER.
I'M FEELING MUCH BETTER. I'D LIKE TO GO BACK TO MY CELL.
BUT... WHAT ABOUT YOUR BRAIN? WHAT IF YOU HAVE A--
WHAT? YOU'RE WORRIED I'M GOING TO DIE FROM A BLOODY NOSE?
THERE REALLY ISN'T ANY KIND OF IQ TEST TO JOIN THE FORCE, IS THERE?
YOU CAME BACK?
OF COURSE. I'D NEVER LEAVE YOU, OZZY.
AND YOU BROUGHT ME GIFTS?
OKAY.
NOT PRESENTS. PAYMENT. YOU'RE SQUARE NOW.

GCPD.
HEY, HARVEY. YOU LOOK NERVOUS.
SOMETHING ELSE YOU WANT TO GET OFF YOUR CHEST?
NO? FAIR ENOUGH.
WE JUST HAD A COUPLE MORE QUESTIONS.
WANT TO TALK ABOUT THE GET-TOGETHER AT THE WAREHOUSE TWO NIGHTS AGO?
I WASN'T THERE.
YES, YOU WERE...AND SO WAS THE RIDDLER.
WHO TOLD YOU THAT?
DON'T WORRY ABOUT IT.
I WON'T.
BUT YOU SHOULD BECAUSE THEY'RE LYING TO YOU. RIDDLER WASN'T THERE.
SO YOU ADMIT YOU WERE.
FINE. GOOD WORK. YOU CAN ADD ANOTHER CHARGE OF "BEING IN A WAREHOUSE" TO MY ARREST.
BUT RIDDLER WASN'T THERE. HE WAS SUPPOSED TO BE...

THAT'S THE NICE THING ABOUT UNLIMITED POWER. ONE CAN GET WHATEVER THEY WANT.
THESE PETTY DISPUTES ARE BENEATH ME AND SOON YOU ALL WILL BE TOO.
BEHOLD! THE MASTER ENGINE!
WHY ARE YOU HERE ANYWAY, JOKER? WHERE'S THE RIDDLER?
AREN'T YOU THE NOSY ONE, HARVEY? I'M HERE TO HELP OUT BECAUSE HE IS TIED UP WITH OTHER THINGS AT THE MOMENT.
RUMMMMBLE!
IS IT SUPPOSED TO BE DOING THAT?
SMASH!
THE BOX IS GONE! AND SO IS THE JOKER.

"SUDDENLY, YOU-KNOW-WHO SHOWED UP."
EVERYONE HAND OVER YOUR MONEY RIGHT NOW!
"BATMAN WAS THERE TO ROB YOU?"
AHHH!
"HOW DO YOU THINK HE PAYS FOR ALL HIS STUFF?
RUN FOR IT!
PSST. HARV! OVER HERE.
THERE IS A WAY OUT THROUGH HERE.
WHY ARE YOU HELPING ME?
BECAUSE I RESPECT YOU...AND I NEED YOU TO TAKE THIS.
"AND THEN I WENT HOME."
"AND HE JUST GAVE YOU THE BOX, DENT?"
"YES."
"AND WHAT DID YOU DO WITH IT?"
"I THINK THAT'S ENOUGH. ANYTHING ELSE YOU CAN ASK MY LAWYER."

OKAY, PENGUIN. CAN WE--
IT'S **MR. COBBLEPOT,** YOU GLORIFIED GARBAGEMAN.
ON A NIGHT LIKE THIS IT DOESN'T FEEL LIKE THERE IS ANYTHING **GLORIFIED** ABOUT IT.
WE WERE HOPING YOU COULD ANSWER A COUPLE QUESTIONS ABOUT WHAT HAPPENED AT THE WAREHOUSE TWO NIGHTS
NO COMMENT.
LOOK, WE KNOW YOU WERE THERE.
NO COMMENT.
AND THE RIDDLER WAS THERE.
...NO COMMENT.
WHICH MAKES YOU ONE OF THE LAST PEOPLE TO SEE HIM **ALIVE.**
NO COMMENT.
WE'VE HEARD THAT YOU WERE QUITE **UPSET** WITH HIM THAT NIGHT.
NO--WAIT. WHO TOLD YOU THAT? IS IT **BANE?** HE'S A DAMN APE IN A MASK!
WE HAVEN'T SPOKEN TO BANE. **YET.** BUT MR. TETCH HAS BEEN GIVING US A LOT OF USEFUL INFORMATION--
HA!
THE **MAD HATTER** IS YOUR WITNESS?
THE MAN BELIEVES HE LIVES **INSIDE A CHILDREN'S BOOK.** WELL DONE.
FOR THE RECORD, THE RIDDLER WASN'T EVEN THERE THAT NIGHT.

HEE-HEE! I WILL HAVE LOTS OF POWER, FOR WHATEVER I WANT.
HA! I'M SICK OF EVERYONE ARGUING. I ALWAYS LOSE. TEE-HEE!
NOW LOOK AT THE MASTER ENGINE!
"YOU'RE SAYING IT WAS THE JOKER COORDINATING THINGS THAT NIGHT? AND THE RIDDLER WASN'T EVER THERE, COBBLEPOT?"
"YES."
SHOULDN'T IT DO SOMETHING?
HA!
"ARE YOU SURE?"
"AM I A @!#$%&* MORON? OF COURSE I'M SURE."
IT'S FAKE, YOU WEED.
YOU WERE TRICKED, JUST LIKE THAT GORILLA BANE! HEE-HEE!
OSWALD?
I KNEW YOU COULD DO IT.
DON'T SUCK UP TO ME, CLOWN. I DON'T LIKE YOU.
SORRY. HA!
CLIC!
OH, WHAT DID YOU DO NOW, YOU SIMPLETON?

SMASH!
WHAT'S GOING ON?
THE JOKER ABSCONDED.
"AND THEN THE CURSED BAT SHOWED UP."
DIE, APE!
AHHH! HELP ME, PLEASE!
THAT'S ENOUGH, DEVIANT!
WHAP!
"ARE YOU TELLING ME--"
"YOU WANT ME TO FINISH MY @#$%!*& STORY OR NOT?"

"I WATCHED ALL OF THEM SCATTER LIKE RATS IN A BURNING BUILDING.
"BUT I KNEW ONLY ONE RAT WOULD DEFINITELY KNOW THE WAY OUT."
"SO YOU RAN. ALL THAT FOR NOTHING, EH OSWALD?"
"NOT EXACTLY, DETECTIVE.
HERE! HEE-HEE! I DON'T FEEL SAFE WITH IT.
"I GOT THE MASTER ENGINE, WHICH WAS RIGHTFULLY MINE ANYWAY."
"YOU HAVE IT?"
BUT IT'S NOTHING MORE THAN A NICE ANTIQUITY FOR MY MANTLE. IT DOESN'T DO ANYTHING.

DR. QUINZEL--
IT'S QUINN.
NO. IT ISN'T.
YOU CAN CALL ME WHATEVER YA WANT IF IT MAKES YA FEEL BETTER ABOUT YOURSELF, BIG GUY.
WE APPRECIATE THAT, MS. QUINN. NOW WE KNOW YOU'RE GOING TO DENY KNOWING ANYTHING ABOUT IT...
...BUT WE WANTED TO ASK SOME QUESTIONS ABOUT THE MEETING AT THE WAREHOUSE TWO NIGHTS AGO.
OKAY. WHADDAYA WANNA KNOW?
IT WAS A REAL CRAPPY NIGHT. I WENT TO MEET WITH ALL THE RIDDLER'S LITTLE BOY ARMY. BIG BABY BANE, SCARY MASK MAN, PROFESSOR PIGGLY WIGGLY... WHAT'S HIS FACE? THAT BUTTERFLY GUY?
YOU MEAN KILLER--
YEAH! KILLER BUTTERFLY. HIM. HE WAS LATE THOUGH. NEVER HIRE A BUTTERFLY TO DO A CRIMINAL'S JOB.
THAT'S WHAT MY NANA USED TO SAY. PROBABLY. WE WEREN'T CLOSE.
SO THE RIDDLER WAS THERE--
HE WASN'T EVEN THERE, CAN YOU BELIEVE IT? WHOLE PARTY IS HIS IDEA AND HE DOESN'T SHOW. NEVER HIRE A GUY WHO LIKES WORD GAMES TO DO A CRIMINAL'S JOB. MY GRANPA DID USED TO SAY THAT. NEVER GOT IT UNTIL NOW.

"BUT THEN SELINA BROUGHT ALL THESE OTHER BOYS TO THE PARTY. IT WOULDN'T BE A BIG DEAL BUT OF COURSE WITH THESE TYPES *EVERYTHING* IS A BIG DEAL.
"YOU DON'T KNOW WHAT IT'S LIKE. YOU CAN'T EVER HAVE A GET-TOGETHER WITH YOUR PEERS WITHOUT SOMEONE GETTING EXCITED ABOUT MURDER. WAIT, YOU'RE COPS. MAYBE YOU DO KNOW WHAT THAT'S LIKE.
10
"BUT IT WAS A PRETTY NORMAL NIGHT. WELL, NORMAL FOR ME. YOU GUYS'D BE CRYIN'.
BLAH BLAH BLAH... TOXIC MASCULINITY. I'M A BORING AND JUVENILE ATTEMPT AS SEEMING BOTH CRAZY AND EDGY. LIFE'S ALL A JOKE *AND* ONLY I GET IT. ISN'T THAT COOL AND UNIQUE? AREN'T I *MISUNDERSTOOD?*
"I'LL TELL YA, I *WISH* EDDY WAS THERE. BUT INSTEAD, THE JOKER SHOWS UP TO RUN THINGS. YOU GUYS KNOW HE'S A REAL PIECE OF $#!%, RIGHT?"
"YEAH, WE PICKED UP ON THAT, MS. QUINN."
"YOU SAY THAT. BUT YOU'RE COPS. YOU THINK WE *ALL* SUCK. BUT HE *REALLY* SUCKS. LIKE BANE? *SO* POLITE. AND MR. FREEZE? SUCH A SWEETIE. EVEN SCARECROW IS PRETTY FUNNY.
"BUT JOKER? JUST SUCKS.
"I WAS THINKING OF JUST TAKING HIM OUT. LIKE, YA KNOW, FOR THE GOOD OF MANKIND OR WHATEVER. YOU GUYS WOULDN'T HAVE CARED. I PROLLY WOULDA DONE IT IF HE DIDN'T HAVE THAT ALLIGATOR THERE."
"DO YOU MEAN... *KILLER CROC?*"
"YEAH. I DON'T LIKE HAVING TO DO WORK STUFF WITH AN ALLIGATOR WATCHING ALL THE TIME. UNPREDICTABLE."
"HE'S NOT AN ACTUAL ALLIGATOR. YOU GET THAT, RIGHT? HE'S LIKE A GUY WITH BAD TEETH AND A SKIN CONDITION. HIS NAME IS WAYLON."
"NO. I DON'T THINK SO, OFFICER.
"ANYWAY, IVY FINALLY SOLVED THE BIG *RUBIK'S CUBE* OR WHATEVER, BECAUSE OF COURSE SHE DID. THAT GIRL IS SOMETHIN' ELSE.
"BUT WOULDN'T YA KNOW IT, IT WAS SOME KINDA *TRICK*.
BLAM!
BLAM!
YAIEEEE!
"THEN THE LIGHTS WENT OUT. SOMEBODY SHOT SOMEBODY. SOME LADY SCREAMED. SHE SOUNDED REAL UPSET. DID YOU TALK TO HER? IS SHE OKAY?"
"SHE'S FINE."
"GOOD."

"AND WHEN WE COULD SEE AGAIN WE SAW THE JOKER WAS GONE AND THE JUSTICE LEAGUE WAS PLAYING CATCH WITH OSWALD. AGAIN.
SOMEBODY HELP ME! I'M PEEING MYSELF!
TOSS HIM OVER HERE. I'M GONNA EAT HIM.
WAIT, REALLY?
SURE. I'M, LIKE, AN ALIEN, RIGHT? WHY NOT?
"SO WE ALL TOOK OFF RUNNING TO GET AWAY. IT'S LIKE THAT OLD JOKE ABOUT CAMPING IN BEAR COUNTRY.
"YOU DON'T HAVE TO BE FASTER THAN A BEAR.
"YOU JUST HAVE TO BE FASTER THAN YOUR FRIENDS.
"ONLY MY BEAR IS A BAT... AND I HATE MY FRIENDS.
"AND WHILE I'M LOOKING FOR A WAY OUT OF THIS WEIRD WAREHOUSE THAT SEEMS TO ONLY EXIST FOR BAD GUYS TO HANG OUT IN, I SEE THE JOKER HANDING THE MAGIC BOX TO THE MAD HATTER OF ALL PEOPLE.
"PERVERTS LOVE PERVERTS."
"THEN WHAT HAPPENED, MS. QUINN?"
GIVE ME THE MAGICAL BOX, YOU TINY PIECE OF @#*$!
"I KICKED HIS BOOTY AND TOOK IT."
"YOU JUST BEAT HIM UP AND TOOK IT?"
WHOK!
"YEAH? THAT'S NOT A CRIME."
"NO. IT MOST DEFINITELY IS. A FEW ACTUALLY."
"WELL, I'M NOT GONNA PRESS CHARGES ON THE LITTLE CREEP."
"IS THAT...IS THAT THE END OF THE STORY?"
"YUP."
"THANK GOD. SO YOU'RE TELLING US YOU HAVE THE BOX?"
"...MAYBE?"

IF IT WERE UP TO ME, THE HATTER WOULD GO FREE.
HEYA, JERVIS. WE ACTUALLY WANT TO ASK YOU A FEW MORE QUESTIONS.
OH, NO.
TWO NIGHTS AGO AT THE WAREHOUSE--
I WASN'T THERE.
WE KNOW YOU WERE. DON'T LIE TO US. ALL WE WANT TO KNOW IS IF YOU SAW THE RIDDLER THERE.
THIS ISN'T FAIR. TALKING TO YOU PUTS ME IN DANGER.
YOU'RE ASKING ME TO GO OUT ON A LIMB FOR YOU?
NO, HE WASN'T THERE. I SWEAR THAT THIS IS TRUE.

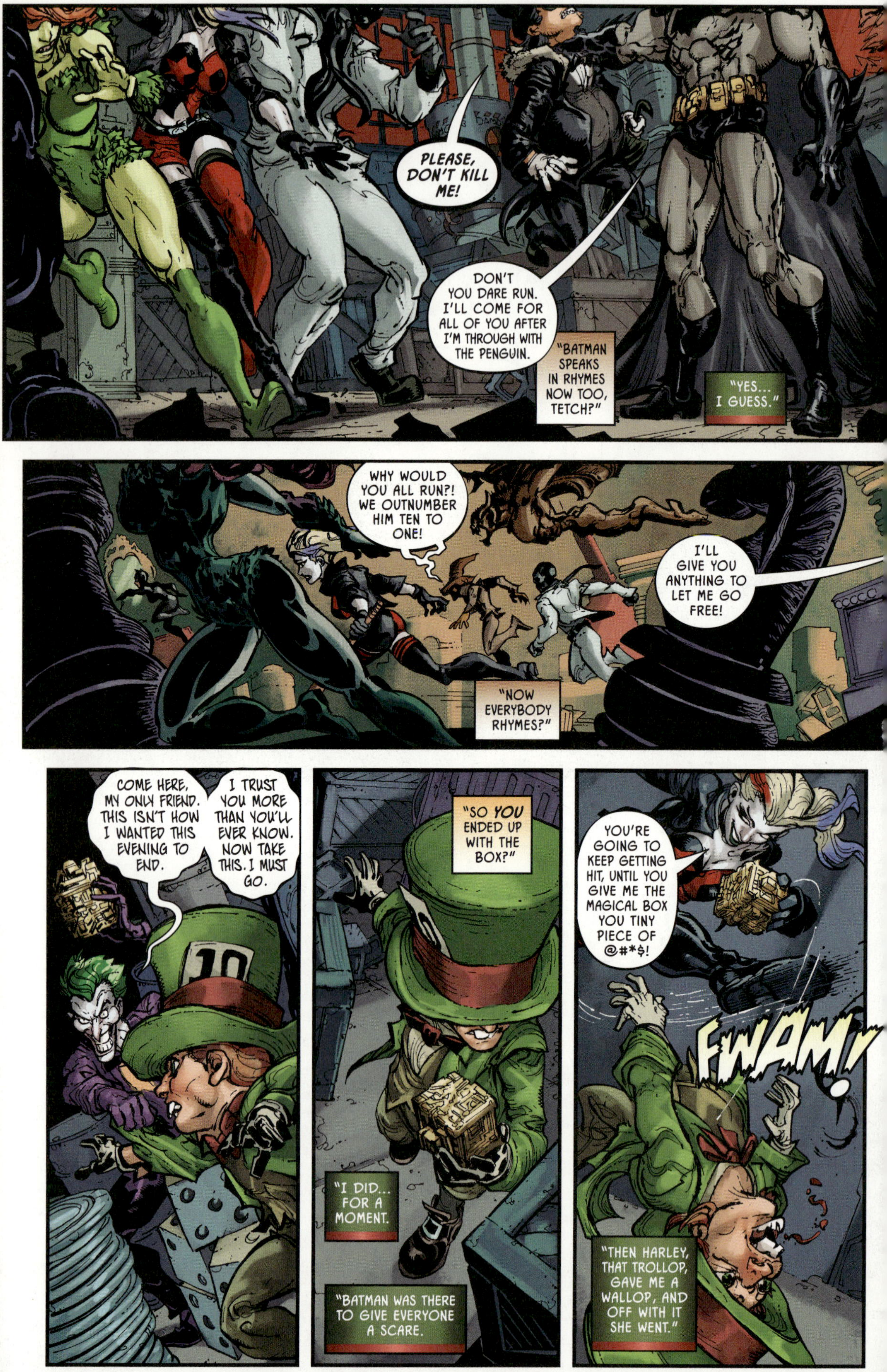
PLEASE, DON'T KILL ME!
DON'T YOU DARE RUN. I'LL COME FOR ALL OF YOU AFTER I'M THROUGH WITH THE PENGUIN.
"BATMAN SPEAKS IN RHYMES NOW TOO, TETCH?"
"YES... I GUESS."
WHY WOULD YOU ALL RUN?! WE OUTNUMBER HIM TEN TO ONE!
I'LL GIVE YOU ANYTHING TO LET ME GO FREE!
"NOW EVERYBODY RHYMES?"
COME HERE, MY ONLY FRIEND. THIS ISN'T HOW I WANTED THIS EVENING TO END.
I TRUST YOU MORE THAN YOU'LL EVER KNOW. NOW TAKE THIS. I MUST GO.
"SO YOU ENDED UP WITH THE BOX?"
"I DID... FOR A MOMENT.
"BATMAN WAS THERE TO GIVE EVERYONE A SCARE.
YOU'RE GOING TO KEEP GETTING HIT, UNTIL YOU GIVE ME THE MAGICAL BOX YOU TINY PIECE OF @#*$!
FWAM!
"THEN HARLEY, THAT TROLLOP, GAVE ME A WALLOP, AND OFF WITH IT SHE WENT."

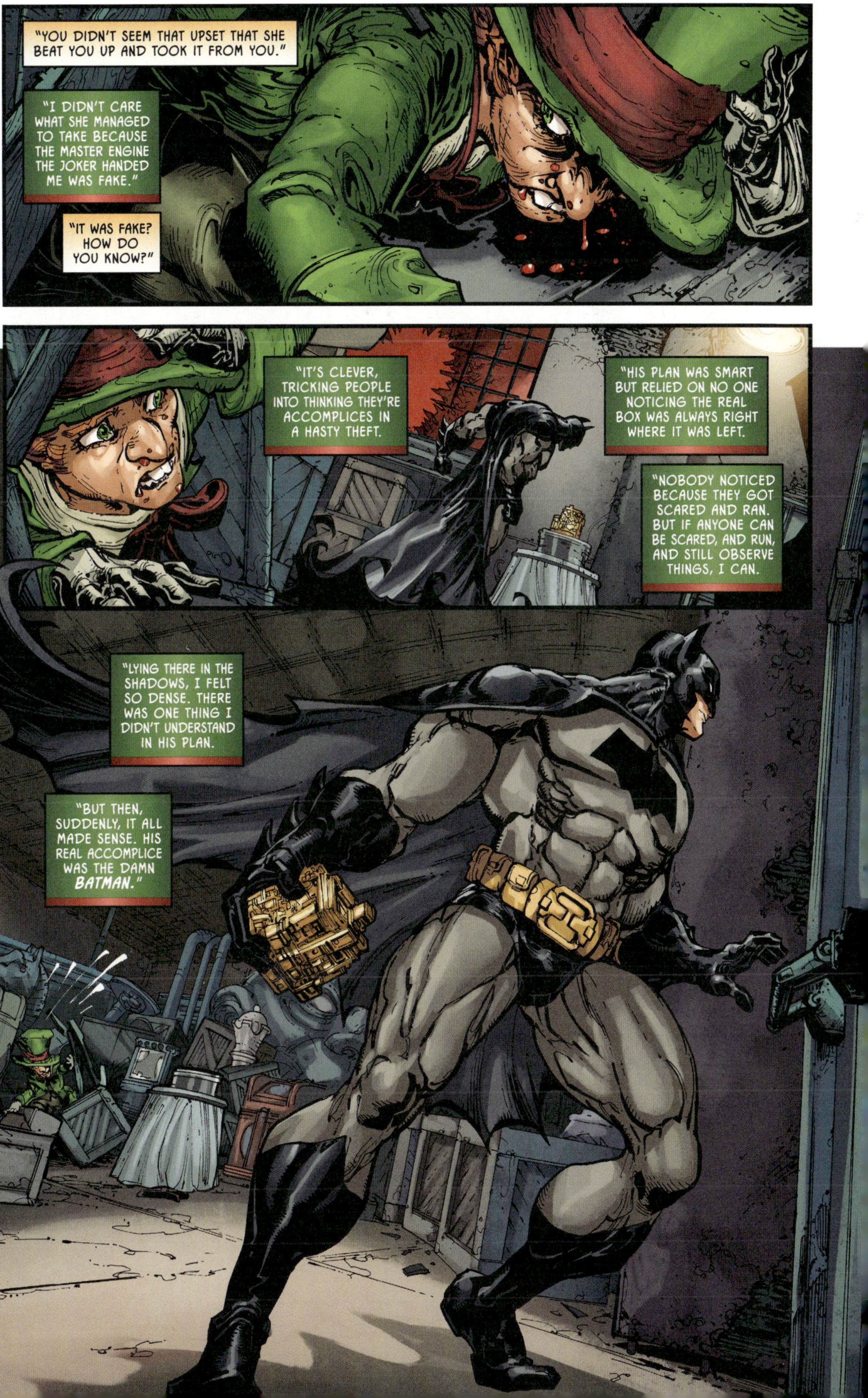
"YOU DIDN'T SEEM THAT UPSET THAT SHE BEAT YOU UP AND TOOK IT FROM YOU."
"I DIDN'T CARE WHAT SHE MANAGED TO TAKE BECAUSE THE MASTER ENGINE THE JOKER HANDED ME WAS FAKE."
"IT WAS FAKE? HOW DO YOU KNOW?"
"IT'S CLEVER, TRICKING PEOPLE INTO THINKING THEY'RE ACCOMPLICES IN A HASTY THEFT.
"HIS PLAN WAS SMART BUT RELIED ON NO ONE NOTICING THE REAL BOX WAS ALWAYS RIGHT WHERE IT WAS LEFT.
"NOBODY NOTICED BECAUSE THEY GOT SCARED AND RAN. BUT IF ANYONE CAN BE SCARED, AND RUN, AND STILL OBSERVE THINGS, I CAN.
"LYING THERE IN THE SHADOWS, I FELT SO DENSE. THERE WAS ONE THING I DIDN'T UNDERSTAND IN HIS PLAN.
"BUT THEN, SUDDENLY, IT ALL MADE SENSE. HIS REAL ACCOMPLICE WAS THE DAMN *BATMAN.*"

A FEW MINUTES AGO.
HEY, BACHMAN! WE GOT ANY DONUTS IN HERE?
GCPD
GOTHNUTS
NO... I MEAN, YEAH BUT...
...I'M SUPPOSED TO BRING THEM TO SEFERT. THEY GOT HIM STUCK GUARDING A DOOR IN THE BASEMENT.
AND YOU'RE GONNA BRING HIM DONUTS FOR LUNCH? GO GET HIM A SANDWICH OR SOMETHING.
BESIDES, NONE OF US SHOULD BE EATING THIS STUFF. LOOKS LIKE WE GOT RATS AGAIN.
GCPD
GOTHNUTS
WHAT THE HELL IS THIS?
WE GOTTA PUT HIM IN THE SOLITARY HOLDING CELL. HE WAS TRYING TO EAT THE CAT LADY.
NO @#$&. AND YOU STOPPED HIM?
I NEED THESE.
@#$& YOU. I NEED THEM FOR THE JOKER.
@#$& THE JOKER. OUR GUY'S GONNA TALK.
...DON'T LIE ABOUT ME!

HERE, WAYLON. WE GOT YOU SOME FOOD.
NOW YOU'LL ANSWER SOME OF OUR QUESTIONS?
Munch! Munch!
YEAH.
WHEN DID YOU FIRST HEAR ABOUT THE MASTER ENGINE BOX?
Munch! Munch!
NEVER HEARD OF IT.
Munch! Munch!
WITNESSES SAID YOU HAD A PIECE OF IT.
THEY'RE LYING?
Munch! Munch!
YEAH.
Munch! Munch!
OKAY. THEN WHY'D YOU GO TO THAT WAREHOUSE WHERE THEY WERE ASSEMBLING IT TWO NIGHTS AGO?
Munch! Munch!
I DIDN'T.
Munch! Munch!
FINE. DO YOU KNOW WHO KILLED THE RIDDLER?
Munch! Munch!
WHO?
Munch! Munch!

THANKS SO MUCH FOR YOUR COOPERATION, WAYLON. YOU WERE A BIG HELP.
ANYTIME.
HEY, BULLOCK, WHAT THE HELL JUST HAPPENED OUT HERE?
THAT PYG GUY GOT LOOSE AND GRABBED SOME ROOKIE'S GUN.
RAN UP TO THE ROOF.
NO @#!$. YOU GO AFTER HIM?
ARE YOU KIDDING? I WENT AND TOOK A LEAK. ROOKIES WANT TO LOSE HIM, THEY CAN BRING HIM BACK.
DID THEY?
NAH. THE DAMN BAT ASSAULTED HIM ON THE ROOF.
FIGURES.
HEY, YOU EAT ALL MY DONUTS?
ONE LEFT.
PERFECT.
Next: TONIGHT! THERE'S GONNA BE A JAILBREAK!

The Joker Presents: A Puzzlebox #6 cover by CHIP ZDARSKY

GCPD.
IT'S ALL &@!?$#*%, JOKER.
EVERY SINGLE WORD YOU'VE SAID.
I DON'T THINK YOU BELIEVE THAT, ADMIRAL GORDON.
GIVE ME ONE REASON WHY I SHOULDN'T JUST THROW YOU BACK IN THAT CELL WITH ALL THOSE MONSTERS WHO WANT TO TEAR YOU APART.
TRYING TO SCARE ME WITH YOUR MONSTERS, JIM BOY?
DON'T YOU UNDERSTAND? I AM WHAT KEEPS THOSE MONSTERS UP AT NIGHT.
OH... I SUPPOSE YOU WANT ME TO LET HIM GO?
CLICK!
AT THIS POINT I'M HOPING YOU DON'T. THIS ROOM COULD USE A NEW COAT OF PAINT.
HOW THE HELL DID YOU GET OUT OF YOUR CUFFS?
WAS I SUPPOSED TO KEEP WEARING THOSE? THEY WERE STARTING TO CHAFE.
NOT TOO TIGHT NOW. I'M--
OWW. I THOUGHT WE WERE JUST HAVING FUN.
HALF A DOZEN WITNESSES PUT YOU AT THE WAREHOUSE TWO NIGHTS AGO. NOT THE RIDDLER.
CLACK!
THESE WITNESSES, THEY ARE YOUR AFOREMENTIONED MONSTERS? FEELS FLIMSY, JIMOTHY.

TWO NIGHTS AGO. GOTHAM. A BAD PART OF TOWN.
THE JOKER PRESENTS: A PUZZLEBOX
"BUT RATHER THAN LISTEN TO YOUR SILLY THEORIES, WHY DON'T I GET TO THE POINT."
SLOW DOWN, MA'AM. JUST TELL US WHAT YOU SAW.
ALL THESE PEOPLE DRESSED SO STRANGELY. I THOUGHT IT WAS A COSTUME PARTY. BUT THEN THE MAN IN THE GREEN SUIT...
OH, GOD. THEY HURT HIM. HE LEFT BUT HE WAS HURT BAD.
WHO HURT HIM?
I DON'T KNOW THEIR NAME. THEY'RE STILL IN THERE I THINK.
POLICE
SHOULD WE GO IN?
YOU SUICIDAL NOW, BILL?
CALL DISPATCH AND TELL THEM WE NEED EVERYONE THEY CAN SPARE.
NOW.
SOMEONE'S COMING OUT.
The Freezing Point of Clay
IS THAT...?
HEY! BATMAN!
IS HE... RUNNING FROM US?
YUP.
IS THAT NORMAL?
I HAVE NO IDEA.

A LITTLE WHILE LATER. A DIFFERENT BAD PART OF THE SAME BAD TOWN.
"YOU'RE TELLING US BATMAN STOLE THIS MAGICAL CUBE--"
"THE MASTER ENGINE."
"HE STOLE IT AND RAN AWAY FROM THE POLICE ON SITE?"
KNOCK KNOCK?
MATTHEW ROSENBERG writer
JUAN DOE, JESÚS MERINO & VICENTE CIFUENTES artists
SHAWN CRYSTAL layouts pgs 2-10
VICENTE CIFUENTES finishes pgs 2-10
JUAN DOE & ULISES ARREOLA colors
FERRAN DELGADO letterer
BATMAN created by BOB KANE with BILL FINGER
ANYBODY HOME?
"IT SOUNDS ABSURD WHEN YOU SAY IT, JAMES. BUT I'M SURE THE RESPONDING OFFICERS WOULD HAVE FILED A REPORT ON THAT, RIGHT?
"AND YOU WOULD HAVE READ THAT BY NOW TOO, RIGHT? SO YOU'D KNOW IF I WAS LYING, YES? NOW MAY I CONTINUE?"
"GO ON."
HMM... SEEMS LIKE A LOT OF TROUBLE TO GO THROUGH TO GET ANOTHER ONE OF THESE.

THAT ONE IS FAKE, BATMAN.
I COULD TELL. IT'S MUCH LIGHTER. LIKE IT'S HOLLOW.
IS IT?
WOULD YOU MIND CHANGING OUT OF THAT RIDICULOUS GETUP? YOU'RE MAKING ME UNCOMFORTABLE.
THAT BETTER?
MUCH.
YOUR TURN. YOU WANT TO STEP OUT HERE SO I CAN SEE WHO I'VE BEEN DEALING WITH?
FAIR ENOUGH, CLAYFACE. I GUESS YOU'VE EARNED THAT.

TA-DA!
YOU?! I WAS WORKING FOR YOU THIS WHOLE TIME?
YOU WERE. AND THANK YOU.
I DON'T LIKE BEING TRICKED.
MOST PEOPLE DON'T. BUT YOUR SERVICE PROVED INVALUABLE TO ME.
"IS THIS A JOKE? YOU'RE NOT GOING TO TELL US WHO HIRED HIM, JOKER?"
"I DON'T KNOW, JAMES. NEVER SAW THEM."
I NEEDED SOMEONE STUPID, AND MALLEABLE, WHO COULD GET ME EVERYTHING I NEEDED.
WHO FITS THAT BILL BETTER THAN YOU?
YOU SHOULDN'T TALK TO ME LIKE THAT...
DON'T GET ALL WORKED UP NOW. HUFFING AND PUFFING.
SAY... I CAN'T SEE YOUR BREATH?
WHAT?
A PERSON COULD GET PRETTY COLD STAYING HERE TOO LONG, COULDN'T THEY?
I... DON'T FEEL IT.
OF COURSE YOU DON'T. BECAUSE YOU'RE NOT QUITE A PERSON.
WE'RE DONE HERE, RIGHT?
JUST ABOUT. I STILL HAVE TO PAY FOR SERVICES RENDERED.
DON'T WORRY. YOU CAN PAY ME LATER.
I DIDN'T MEAN YOU...

...I MEANT HIM.
RAWR
KZZT!
MR. FREEZE ASSURED ME THAT DISPOSING OF YOU WAS GOING TO BE A BORE, CLAYFACE.
BUT THIS IS FUN!

CAREFUL, GENTLEMEN.
I'D HATE TO HAVE TO TRY AND FIND ANOTHER DAMN MAGICAL CUBE.
ANY LAST WORDS, BASIL?
UUUHH KIII BWWW
TYPICAL.
KZZT!
THERE. I THINK WE ARE FINISHED HERE.
NOW, ABOUT MY PAYMENT...

PTOOO!
AAARGH!
YOU CELEBRATED TOO SOON, VICTOR.
WHROOMM!
YOU ALWAYS WERE SHORTSIGHTED.
KZZT!
A LITTLE COLD WON'T STOP ME NOW.
SLASHH!
DON'T BREAK THE MERCHANDISE, VICTOR.

GAH! I'LL KILL YOU BOTH!
A BOLD CLAIM FOR SOMEONE WHO JUST GOT BABY ARMED IN A FIGHT.
THE BABY ARM IS SO DIVINELY GROSS.
FOR A MAN THAT APPEARS TO BE MADE OF EXCREMENT, I AM IMPRESSED HOW YOU CONTINUE TO FIND NEW WAYS TO REVOLT ME.
AT LEAST I CAN KILL YOU!!
UMM... VICTOR? MIGHT BE A GOOD TIME TO FINISH THIS?
VICTOR, YOU MORON?!
TIME TO DIE, C--
DO NOT EVER SPEAK TO ME THAT WAY AGAIN.
RIGHT. OF COURSE.
IMPRESSIVE WORK, BY THE WAY. HOW LONG WILL HE STAY LIKE THIS?
I DO NOT KNOW. WITH A NORMAL PERSON IT TAKES BETWEEN THREE AND FIVE DAYS TO THAW. BUT HE IS FAR FROM NORMAL.
NO, HE'S NOT. HE'S A MONSTER... LIKE YOU.
DO NOT PLAY YOUR GAMES WITH ME. UNLIKE POOR BASIL HERE, I AM NOT AFRAID OF YOU. SO CHOOSE YOUR NEXT WORDS WISELY.
PAYMENT. MY NEXT WORD IS PAYMENT. AS IN, GETTING YOU YOURS.

YOU KNOW I MEANT "MONSTERS" LOVINGLY, RIGHT? THE FREAKS. THE MISUNDERSTOOD. OUTCASTS. WE'RE ALL MONSTERS IN THE EYES OF SOCIETY.
I AM NOT.
OF COURSE NOT. MY MISTAKE.
I WILL TAKE THIS AS MY PAYMENT.
HEH. NOW VICTOR, WE ALREADY AGREED ON A PRICE.
THIS IS WHAT YOU WANT.
THE NAMES AND PRICES OF EVERY POLITICIAN, JUDGE, POLICE OFFICER, BUYER, AND SELLER IN THIS LITTLE TOWN.
THIS IS DENT'S?
IT WAS. BUT HE WON'T BE NEEDING IT VERY SOON.
SO BE IT. I WILL TAKE IT BECAUSE I DO NOT LIKE DENT.
AND I DON'T LIKE YOU EITHER. DO NOT CONTACT ME AGAIN.
THAT WAS COLD, VICTOR.
BESIDES, I HAVE WORK TO DO. RIGHT, BASIL?

GCPD.
YOU'RE A @!$%&@# MORON!
I'M JUST SAYING, ARE YOU SURE THE JOKER'S NOT A COP?
AND I'M SAYING YOU'RE A @!$%&@# MORON.
HE'S SAYING WHO KNOWS WHAT WHILE WE'RE ALL STUCK IN HERE.
THAT'S YOUR WHOLE THEORY, KILLER MOTH?!? YOU GOT ARRESTED, SO THE JOKER MUST BE A POLICE OFFICER?
NOT JUST ME. ALL OF US. HELL, EVEN FREEZE OVER THERE IS GOING DOWN AND I DON'T THINK HE HAD ANYTHING TO DO WITH ANY OF THIS.
HE'S JUST ANOTHER IDIOT THE JOKER GOT LOCKED UP.
I DIDN'T MEAN THE IDIOT THING. I'M SURE YOU'RE REAL SMART. I JUST MEANT ALL THE FREAKS ARE GETTING LOCKED UP...
WAIT...
KEEP GOING. THIS IS WONDERFUL.
I DON'T WANT TO HAVE TO FIGHT YOU, MAN...
OH, THANK GOD.
JAILER, I WISH TO SPEAK.

JEAN, THIS GUY WANTS TO TALK. CAN WE PUT HIM IN BOX THREE?
NO. THE MAD HATTER'S IN THERE.
I THINK TWO IS OPEN.
WHERE IS THE JOKER?
HE'S IN ONE.
FSSSSSSSSSSSSS
BUSY, HUH?
YEAH. I'VE NEVER SEEN IT LIKE THIS BEFORE.
AAAHHHH...
FSSSSSSSSSSSSS
WHAT THE HELL...?!
AHHHH...
HIS SUIT IS LEAKING!
GET AN AMBULANCE!
THEY'RE NOT GOING TO KNOW WHAT TO DO WITH HIM. WE NEED TO GET HIM SOMEWHERE COLD, RIGHT? OR HE'LL DIE?
FSSSSSSSSSSSSS

KRASH!
Squeek Squeek Squeek
FREEZE! WHAT ARE YOU DOING?!
TURN AROUND SLOWLY OR I WILL BE FORCED TO SHOOT!
FREEZE, STOP RIGHT NOW!
fsssssssssss
I'M AFRAID I CANNOT DO THAT.
SWOOOSH!

BLAM! BLAM! BLAM!
MY QUARREL IS NOT WITH ANY OF YOU.
REMEMBER THAT WHEN YOU STIR AWAKE IN THE HOSPITAL OR LIE STILL IN THE MORGUE.
KZZZT!
THAT'S BETTER.
A RESPECTFUL AMOUNT OF INTIMIDATION FROM BOTH PARTIES IS WHERE WE ARE AT OUR MOST COMFORTABLE, ISN'T IT.
DO NOT BOTHER TRYING TO SHUT OFF THE WATER. I HAVE FROZEN THE VALVE, MAKING IT IMPOSSIBLE...
...SO IT'S BEST TO SIMPLY ALLOW ME TO PROCEED WITH MY PLAN.

DID I EVER TELL YOU ABOUT THE TIME THAT THE RIDDLER TRIED TO MURDER THE MAYOR USING TRAINED RACCOONS?
THAT WAS YOU.
WAS IT?
JOKER! IT IS TIME FOR YOU TO MEET YOUR MAKER.
DROP IT, FREEZE!
YOU TRIED TO TRICK ME. DID YOU THINK THERE WOULD NOT BE CONSEQUENCES?
NICE HOSE, VICTOR.
I WOULD THINK YOU'D BE MORE EXCITED TO SEE ME THOUGH.
I TEND TO NOT REALLY THINK THAT FAR IN ADVANCE.
NOW WOULD BE A GOOD TIME TO SHUT YOUR MOUTH.
OH, CALM DOWN, JIMMY.
HE KNOWS THIS WILL ALL BE OVER SOON AND I WILL BE ABLE TO MAKE IT ALL BETTER, SO HE ISN'T GOING TO KILL ME. ISN'T THAT RIGHT, VICTOR?
CLUNK!
NO. I AM.

MMM. THAT HAD NOT OCCURRED TO ME.
WHO WAS IN CHARGE OF TAKING THESE GUYS' WEAPONS AWAY?
IT'S NOT A WEAPON, HARVEY. HE WAS USING THE COOLANT FROM HIS SUIT. HE NEEDS IT TO LIVE.
CAN'T NEED IT THAT MUCH IF HE WAS WILLING TO USE IT TO FREEZE THE JOKER HERE.
NO, HE DOES. HE WAS LITERALLY KILLING HIMSELF TO KILL ME.
WHAT AN AMAZING MAN.

GCPD.
WHERE ARE THEY TAKING HIM?
HOPEFULLY OUT BACK TO BE SHOT.
I DIDN'T KNOW WE WERE GOING ON A FIELD TRIP, ADMIRAL GORDON. I DIDN'T BRING MY PERMISSION SLIP.
YOU JUST LOVE PLAYING GAMES.
GUILTY AS CHARGED.
SO ARE WE DONE HERE? YOU'RE LETTING ME GO?
NOT QUITE.

I'M NOT SURE WHAT HELP I COULD BE TO YOU IN THE *BASEMENT*.
ARE YOU SURE WE'RE GOING THE RIGHT WAY?
ANYONE BEEN IN HERE, SEFERT?
NO, SIR, COMMISSIONER.
HEY, ANY OF YOU GUYS SEEN *BACHMAN?* HE'S BRINGING ME FOOD.
NO, SORRY.
LAST CHANCE, JOKER. *WHO* KILLED THE *RIDDLER?*
AFTER GOING OVER THE STORY WITH YOU *I* DON'T THINK HE'S DEAD.
I KNOW YOU HAVE THOSE PHOTOS, BUT DON'T YOU THINK IT'S POSSIBLE HE FAKED THOSE? I KNEW A GUY WHO COULD--
--WELL. LOOK AT THAT.
VERY COLD.
JIM, I THINK THIS MAN MIGHT BE *SICK*.

GOTHAM ZOO
"YOU WANT TO KNOW WHAT I THINK HAPPENED TO HIM, JOKER?"
"NOT REALLY."
"YOU FIGURED OUT THAT HE WAS WORKING ON SOME PLAN TO ASSEMBLE THAT MAGICAL BOX.
"SO YOU MET UP WITH HIM."
"I TOLD YOU I DID."
I WANTED TO TALK TO YOU ABOUT MY PROPOSITION, RIDDLER.
YES, I GOT YOUR MESSAGE.
I'M NOT SURE I'M INTERESTED IN DOING BUSINESS WITH A CLOWN, JOKER.
YOU AND ME, WORKING TOGETHER? WE COULD DO AMAZING THINGS.
I ALWAYS DO AMAZING THINGS, JOKER. WHY DO I NEED YOU?
WE'VE ALWAYS BEEN CLOSE.
NO, WE HAVEN'T.
MAYBE NOT. BUT WE ARE KINDRED SPIRITS.
JOKES ARE JUST RIDDLES FOR STUPID PEOPLE, RIGHT? SO IT JUST FEELS LIKE WE SHOULD WORK TOGETHER?
EXACTLY. YOU'RE GOING TO NEED A TEAM FOR THIS.
WE COULD RULE THIS TOWN. WE COULD RULE THE WORLD.
IS THAT IT?
THOK!
MAYBE I WILL. THANKS FOR THE CHAT. I HAVE YOUR RÉSUMÉ ON FILE.
IF YOU DON'T WANT TO WORK WITH ME, YOU CAN JUST SAY--
NO.

"AM I GETTING CLOSE, JOKER?"
"NO, BUT THIS IS FUN. KEEP GOING."
"SO YOU HIRED CATWOMAN TO PUT TOGETHER HER OWN LITTLE TEAM...
"...AND NONE OF THEM KNEW THEY WERE REALLY WORKING FOR YOU.
"BUT OFF THEY WENT TO ROB, BEAT, AND KILL TO GET THOSE PIECES OF YOUR LITTLE PUZZLEBOX. TO VARYING DEGREES OF SUCCESS."
BLAM!

"BUT THAT DIDN'T REALLY MATTER, DID IT? BECAUSE YOU JUST ADJUSTED YOUR PLAN."
"THAT'S NOT SOMETHING I REALLY DO, JIMBO."
"YOU FOUND OUT WHERE THE RIDDLER WAS MEETING HIS TEAM AND YOU GOT THERE FIRST. SO EVERYONE BROUGHT THE PIECES RIGHT TO YOU.
"AND THEN, COINCIDENTALLY...
SMASH!
"...BATMAN ARRIVED."
"ARE YOU IMPLYING I WORKED WITH THE BATMAN TO ROB PEOPLE?
"I'VE MADE QUESTIONABLE CHOICES IN THE PAST, BUT EVEN I HAVE STANDARDS.
"IT'S A WILD STORY, JAMESON. BUT I BELIEVE I MENTIONED THAT WASN'T ME. IT WAS THE RIDDLER WHO WAS THERE THAT NIGHT."
"FINALLY WE AGREE ON SOMETHING. THE RIDDLER WAS THERE."

HELLO, EDWARD. YOU'RE LATE.
JOKER? WHAT THE HELL ARE YOU DOING HERE?
THIS.
"NOW WAIT A SECOND...
HAHA!
"...WHERE ARE YOU GETTING ALL THIS? THAT'S A PRETTY BOLD CLAIM TO MAKE WITHOUT EVEN A WITNESS, GORDON."
BLAM!
"DON'T YOU WORRY YOUR LITTLE HEAD ABOUT THAT."
YAIEEE!
WHAA--?!
WAIT, EDDIE! COME BACK! I MISS YOU!
"FASCINATING WATCHING YOUR BRAIN WORK, BUT QUICK QUESTION HERE, JAM--
DIDN'T YOU SAY I WAS INSIDE WHEN ALL THIS WAS HAPPENING?"
BLAM!

"I'M SO GLAD YOU ASKED, JOKER. BECAUSE THE MAN INSIDE WHO LOOKED LIKE YOU...
YAIEEEE!
SMASH!
"...IS ALSO THE MAN WHO LOOKED LIKE BATMAN.
"YOU HIRED CLAYFACE, THE ONE VILLAIN SUSPICIOUSLY ABSENT TONIGHT, TO PRETEND TO BE BOTH OF YOU."
"THAT IS SUSPICIOUS. BUT LET ME ASK ANOTHER QUESTION. YOU SAID I WORKED WITH TOYMAN BEFORE? WHY?
"SURELY IT CAN'T BE WHAT SO MANY OF THE OTHER WITNESSES MAY HAVE TOLD YOU ALREADY. THAT I WAS GIVING OUT FAKE BOXES HE MADE FOR ME.
"AND WHY WOULD I GIVE OUT FAKE BOXES IF I HAD A FAKE BATMAN TAKE THE REAL ONE?"

"BECAUSE YOU DIDN'T WANT ANYONE ELSE TO FIGURE OUT YOU MADE OFF WITH THE REAL BOX, THE ONE WE NOW HAVE UPSTAIRS IN EVIDENCE WITH YOUR FINGERPRINTS ALL OVER IT."
HEY, !#@? FOR BRAINS...
...REMEMBER US?
"BUT THEY FIGURED IT OUT."
JOKER, WHERE'S THE RIDDLER, YOU @#$?*!& MANIAC?
TIME FOR *PAIN!*
WAIT! I CAN EXPLAIN... I'LL TELL YOU.
"AND *THAT'S* WHEN BATMAN ARRIVED."
SKRASH!
"THE *REAL* ONE OR MY THEORETICAL FAKE ONE?"
"REAL."

"CHAOS ENSUES.
"I BELIEVE YOU SHOT ONE OF MY OFFICERS."
BLAM!
MAKE ONE MOVE, SCUMBAG.
I'D LOVE AN EXCUSE TO PERSONALLY FINISH YOU OFF FOR SHOOTING MY PARTNER.
GO EASY ON ME. I AM MENTALLY UNWELL.
"AND THAT BRINGS US UP TO RIGHT ABOUT NOW."
THAT'S YOUR STORY? NOT QUITE AS FUN AS MINE, WAS IT? I HAVE A FEW NOTES THOUGH.
THERE'S NO MOTIVE. I ALREADY HAD THE BOX.
WE HAVE--
BY YOUR OWN ADMISSION I WAS INSIDE GIVING OUT FAKE BOXES TO THOSE MONSTERS UPSTAIRS WHEN YOU HAVE ME OUTSIDE SHOOTING THE RIDDLER.
GET HIM OUT OF MY SIGHT. NOW!
AND YOU HAVE A DOZEN WITNESSES WHO WOULD SAY SO, BUT NONE WHO SAW ME SHOOT HIM.

"NO WEAPON. NO MOTIVE. AN ALIBI. AND NO WITNESSES. GOOD WORK, JIM."
THANK YOU FOR YOUR PATIENCE, MA'AM. I'M VERY GLAD YOU CAME IN.
OH. I DON'T KNOW HOW HELPFUL I CAN BE.
I'M SURE YOU WILL BE EXTREMELY HELPFUL.
YOU TOLD MY OFFICERS YOU WERE THERE THE NIGHT THE RIDDLER WAS SHOT? AND YOU EVEN LEFT THE TIP THAT HELPED US LOCATE HIS BODY, IS THAT RIGHT?
IT WAS DARK AND HARD TO SEE.
BUT YOU SAID YOU SAW THE MAN WALKING, HEARD HIM SPEAK, THAT YOU COULD IDENTIFY HIM?
YES. I DID. BUT...
BUT WHAT?
WELL, I KNOW FOR SURE IT WASN'T THAT MAN.

LATER.
HE FROZE THE VALVE...
...SO WE COULDN'T SHUT THE HOSE OFF. FIRE DEPARTMENT FINALLY GOT IT SHUT DOWN. BUT WE WON'T HAVE WATER.
IF YOU GOTTA TAKE A LEAK, USE THE DIM SUM PLACE NEXT DOOR.
WONDERFUL.
WATER SHOULD BE BACK ON *TOMORROW.*
OH, AND THE *FIRE MARSHAL* IS LOOKING FOR YOU. HE SAYS SINCE THE WATER'S OFF IT'S *ILLEGAL* FOR US TO BE IN HERE AND WE HAVE TO *EVACUATE* THE BUILDING.

COMMISSIONER. GLAD I FOUND YOU.
AS YOU KNOW, THAT PYG GUY MANAGED TO GET A WEAPON AND FIRED IT OFF A COUPLE TIMES. TURNS OUT HE HIT SOME CABLES IN THE CEILING.
INTERNET'S DOWN. PHONE LINES ARE DOWN. AND WE'RE HAVING SOME ELECTRICAL PROBLEMS.
WONDERFUL.
HE ALSO DAMAGED SOME EVIDENCE AND SPOOKED THE WITNESS TO THAT BANK ROBBERY A COUPLE WEEKS AGO.
IT'S A REAL $#*& SHOW.

COMMISSIONER. GOOD TO SEE YOU, SIR.
JUST TO KEEP YOU UPDATED--
THE QRT OFFICER WHO GOT SHOT IN THE RAID IS OUT OF SURGERY. DOCTORS ARE OPTIMISTIC.
BUT NADLER IS IN THE HOSPITAL NOW BECAUSE HE GOT HIS HANDS FROZEN. JENKINS TOO, WITH BROKEN RIBS FROM THE HOSE.
AND THE CAPTAIN SUSPENDED THE ROOKIE WHO GOT HIS WEAPON STOLEN BY THE PIG MAN.
GOTHAM HARBOR
GOTHAM CITY
WHAT AM I FORGETTING?
HENSHEL GOT HIS FINGER BITTEN OFF BY CROC IN THE SQUAD CAR.
BIVENS IN EVIDENCE GOT SENT HOME AFTER SOME KIND OF CHEMICAL GOT ON HIM FROM THE STUFF THEY COLLECTED AT THE WAREHOUSE.
AND WHAT'S HIS NAME? KLEINSCHMIDT?
RIGHT. HE REQUESTED IMMEDIATE PSYCH LEAVE AFTER THE PYG INCIDENT.
I DOUBT HE'S EVER COMING BACK, IF I'M BEING HONEST, SIR. HE WAS SHOOK.
SO WE'RE BATTERED, BRUISED, AND A LITTLE UNDERSTAFFED, BUT WE'RE GOOD TO HOLD IT DOWN HERE.
YOU CAN COUNT ON US, COMMISSIONER.
WONDERFUL.

COMMISSIONER... WHERE ARE YOU GOING?
EMERGENCY EXIT
SIR, ANYTHING YOU NEED US WORKING ON?
I GUESS IT'S GOING WELL.
ROOF
STAIRS
EXIT

I THOUGHT YOU WERE QUITTING.
I THOUGHT YOU'D BE ASLEEP BY NOW.
JUST FINISHED PATROLLING. IT'S QUIET NOW.
THAT'S BECAUSE ALL THE CRAZY IS HERE.
THANKS FOR ASSISTING MY PEOPLE WITH PYG BEFORE.
HOW'S IT GOING DOWN THERE?
IT'S NOT.

ALL OF THIS, THE FIGHTING, THE ROBBERIES, RIDDLER'S MURDER, IT'S ALL OVER THIS "MASTER ENGINE." WHICH, AS FAR AS ANYONE CAN TELL ME, IS SOME FAKE MAGIC BOX FROM SOME NONSENSE IMAGINARY ALIEN PEOPLE.
THE NEW GODS AREN'T IMAGINARY. I KNOW THEM.
BE THAT AS IT MAY, WE HAD OUR EXPERTS LOOK AT THE BOX. WE TALKED TO HISTORIANS AND SCIENTISTS.
EVEN EVERYONE WE GOT LOCKED UP DOWNSTAIRS AGREED.
THE BOX IS FAKE. IT DOESN'T DO ANYTHING.
JOKER PUT THE WHOLE DAMN THING TOGETHER AS A JOKE.
IT'S A GOOD THEORY.
BUT I MONITOR THE CITY FOR IRREGULAR ENERGY SIGNATURES.
A SHORT BURST OF RADIATION NOT OF TERRESTRIAL ORIGIN, POSSIBLY FROM THE FOURTH WORLD, WAS RELEASED YESTERDAY APPROXIMATELY TWO MILES FROM HERE.
I BELIEVE SOMEONE USED THE MASTER ENGINE LAST NIGHT.
USED IT FOR WHAT?
YOU TELL ME.
WONDERFUL.
Next Issue:
JAILBREAK!

The Joker Presents: A Puzzlebox #7 cover by **CHIP ZDARSKY**

THE JOKER PRESENTS: A PUZZLEBOX
CHAPTER 13: Go out with a bang!
GCPD.
IS THAT IT?
YEAH, WE'RE DONE.
MATTHEW ROSENBERG writer
MIKE NORTON, JESÚS MERINO & VICENTE CIFUENTES artists
ROMAN STEVENS & ULISES ARREOLA colors
FERRAN DELGADO letterer
BATMAN created by BOB KANE with BILL FINGER
I HOPE I WAS HELPFUL. DID YOU SOLVE THE CASE?
DID YOU FIGURE OUT WHO KILLED THE RIDDLER?
YOU WANT TO KNOW THE ANSWER TO WHO KILLED THE RIDDLER?
WHO CARES?
THAT'S THE DAMN ANSWER.
ONE MORE OF YOU LUNATICS OFF THE STREETS AS FAR AS I'M CONCERNED.

THANKS FOR COMING WITH ME, HARVEY.
LATER.
ALWAYS HAPPY TO COME OUT WITH YOU, IF YOU'RE PAYING.
BESIDES, IF I DIDN'T, YOU'D BE WAKING ME UP IN FOUR HOURS TO TELL ME "SOMETHING DIDN'T FEEL RIGHT."
NONE OF THAT FELT RIGHT. IT WAS ALL TOO CLEAN... BUT STILL A MESS.
WE GET HANDED A BUNCH OF THESE GUYS ON A SILVER PLATTER. WE GOT EVIDENCE ON DOZENS OF NEW CRIMES FOR ALL THEM. HELL, WE GOT CONFESSIONS OUT OF HALF OF THEM.
AND WE GOT NOTHING ON THE RIDDLER'S MURDER. WHY IS THAT?
ONLY ONE WHO DIDN'T CONFESS OR GET DIRECTLY IMPLICATED IN ANYTHING ILLEGAL WAS THE JOKER.
PUT ALL THAT ASIDE. YOU KNOW IT AND I KNOW IT. THE JOKER KILLED HIM, RIGHT?
...YES.
BUT HE WANTED TO GET CAUGHT. HE PUT ALL THIS TOGETHER LAST NIGHT TO END UP IN JAIL. WHY?

MAYBE HE HAD A CHANGE OF HEART AND DECIDED TO HELP US CLEAN UP THE STREETS. WE GOT EVERY WACKO IN TOWN IN HOLDING.
INCLUDING HIMSELF?
HE'S DONE WEIRDER. AND THIS LITTLE PAYROLL OF TWO-FACE'S WILL HELP EVEN MORE ONCE WE DECODE IT.
HEY!
THERE ARE PAGES MISSING!
YOU THINK JOKER TORE THEM OUT?
OR ONE OF OUR GUYS. LET'S GET A LIST OF EVERYONE WHO TOUCHED THIS BOOK SINCE THE RAID LAST NIGHT.
IF THEY TORE THE PAGES OUT TO HIDE THE FACT THAT THEY'RE TAKING MONEY...
...THEN MAYBE THEY'RE HELPING THE JOKER FROM THE INSIDE.
GET CLOSE TO THE BOX?
AGREED. BUT WE'RE BACK TO HELPING HIM DO WHAT? WHAT DOES HE WANT THAT'S INSIDE A POLICE PRECINCT?
HE ALREADY HAD THE BOX. BESIDES, I DONT THINK IT DOES ANYTHING.
BATMAN THINKS IT DOES.
AND HE DRESSES UP LIKE A RODENT TO SCARE CRAZY PEOPLE. THE BOX IS AN OLD LEGEND JOKER USED TO GET EVERYONE WORKED UP.
IS IT... THE WITNESS TO THE RIDDLER'S MURDER?
SHE SEEM COMFORTABLE TO YOU? MAYBE ONE OF THE NAMES FROM THE MISSING PAGES GOT TO HER BEFORE WE--
HE WOULDN'T KNOW WHO SHE WAS OR HOW TO FIND HER. WE DID JUST TAKE HER RIGHT TO HIM. BUT SHE SAID HE WASN'T THE KILLER.

BOOUM
JIM!
JIM, WHERE ARE YOU?!
I'M OKAY, HARVEY.

IS EVERYONE OKAY? DON'T MOVE UNTIL YOU'RE SURE NOTHING IS BROKEN. HELP IS ON THE WAY.
MUST HAVE BEEN A BOMB...
...DEAR GOD. ANOTHER ONE! ON THE EAST SIDE.
BOOOM!
POKTIER
ONE WAY
THAT'S IN TRI-CORNER. IT'S ALL THE NEIGHBORHOODS CONTROLLED BY HIS RIVALS. HE'S DOING THIS. HE'S HITTING ALL THEIR HEADQUARTERS.
BOUM!
BOOM!
HOW?!
I DON'T...
THE BOXES! THE FAKE BOXES!
THEY WERE BOMBS!
JIM...
BOOUM!

"...WE HAVE A BOX AT THE PRECINCT!"
ONE WAY
WHOA! YOU CAN'T GO IN THERE COMMISSIONER. IT'S NOT SAFE.
THE WITNESS... THE ELDERLY WOMAN? DID SHE COME OUT YET?
I DON'T KNOW.
WE NEED TO FIND HER--!
NO OFFENSE, BUT LOOK AROUND, SIR. IT'S CHAOS.

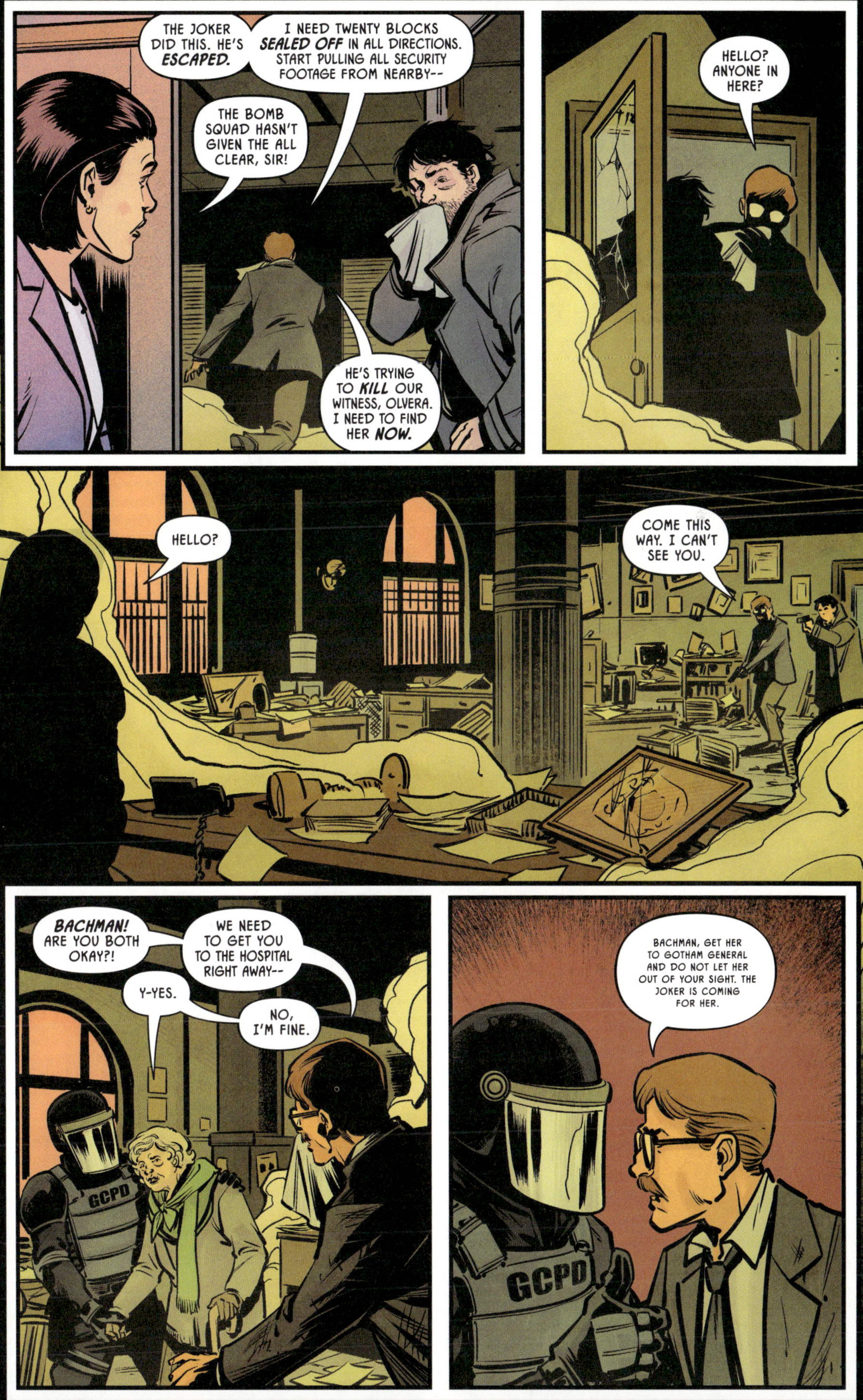
THE JOKER DID THIS. HE'S *ESCAPED.*
I NEED TWENTY BLOCKS *SEALED OFF* IN ALL DIRECTIONS. START PULLING ALL SECURITY FOOTAGE FROM NEARBY--
THE BOMB SQUAD HASN'T GIVEN THE ALL CLEAR, SIR!
HE'S TRYING TO *KILL* OUR WITNESS, OLVERA. I NEED TO FIND HER *NOW.*
HELLO? ANYONE IN HERE?
HELLO?
COME THIS WAY. I CAN'T SEE YOU.
EXIT
BACHMAN! ARE YOU BOTH OKAY?!
WE NEED TO GET YOU TO THE HOSPITAL RIGHT AWAY--
Y-YES.
NO, I'M FINE.
GCPD
BACHMAN, GET HER TO GOTHAM GENERAL AND DO NOT LET HER OUT OF YOUR SIGHT. THE JOKER IS COMING FOR HER.
GCPD

IF SHE WAS STILL IN THE BUILDING HE MAY STILL BE HERE TOO.
LET US OUT, YOU @#$% OF *&%!
WE'RE GONNA DIIIIE!
WHERE DID THE JOKER GO?!
HELLO, COMMISSIONER.
WHAT THE HELL IS GOING ON? HE'S STILL LOCKED UP. IF THE PLAN WAS TO BLOW HER UP SOMETHING WENT WRONG.
HE'S CRAZY BUT NOT SUICIDAL.
THE BOX WASN'T A BOMB?
LET'S GO LOOK.
COME BACK, YOU--!

THERE IS LESS SMOKE ON THIS FLOOR.
GOOD. SOMETHING ABOUT THAT WAS MAKING ME REALLY UNCOMFORTABLE.
ME TOO. BUT IF THE SMOKE ISN'T COMING FROM THE BOX WHERE IS IT COMING FROM?
...AND WHAT WAS IN THE BOX?
COMMISSIONER? CAPTAIN SENT ME TO FIND YOU. BUILDING IS CLEAR BUT YOU STILL PROBABLY SHOULDN'T BE IN HERE UNTIL THE AIR CLEARS.
BOMB IS DEFUSED?
NO INCENDIARIES, SIR. IT WAS A PSYCHEDELIC GAS ATTACK. IT'S DISSIPATING NOW.
WHERE DID IT COME FROM?
YOU'RE NOT GOING TO BELIEVE THIS. IT WAS THE RIDDLER.
WHAT?!
SOMEONE CUT OPEN HIS BODY AND PUT A GAS CANISTER INSIDE. SOMETHING SET IT OFF--
JIM!
IS THAT...?
BACHMAN.

"IF THIS IS BACHMAN THAN WHO THE @#$% WAS THAT DOWNSTAIRS?"
CAN I TAKE THIS DAMN THING OFF NOW?
OF COURSE, MY DEAR.
I DON'T KNOW HOW BLACK MASK DOES THIS ALL THE TIME.
HE'S ONE OF THE CRAZIES, PUNCHLINE MY LOVE.
OH, YES. THAT'S RIGHT. AND WHO ARE WE AGAIN?
WE'RE WHOEVER WE WANT TO BE.

I THINK I'M ABOUT DONE HERE.
GCPD.
DEATHSTROKE, IF YOU WOULDN'T MIND COLLECTING OUR PACKAGE AND CLOSING THE DOOR BEHIND YOU.
OF COURSE.
OUT OF MY WAY!
WE DON'T HAVE MUCH TIME BEFORE THE PIGS COME BACK IN.
LET ME FIND THE PIGS!
CAN'T LET YOU LEAVE. SORRY.
GRRRRR...
WHY NOT?
BECAUSE THAT WASN'T PART OF THE JOB.
NOBODY LEAVES BUT US AND HIM.

CLACK!
WHAT'S THE PLAN
WHILE EVERYONE WAITS OUT *FRONT* FO THE ALL CLEA WE'LL SLIP OUT THE *BACK*.
THAT'S IT?
SIMPLE I *SMART*.
AFTER YOU, *MR. WILSON*.
HA!
I DID NOT EXPECT *THAT*.
THROK!

GOOD MORNING, BATMAN--
THWAP!
THAT'S OUR CUE TO LEAVE.
I WANT TO SEE HOW THIS TURNS OUT.
I'VE SEEN IT BEFORE. IT DOESN'T END THE WAY YOU WANT. LET'S GO.
WHAM!
WE GOT MOVEMENT IN THE BUILDING!
LET'S TRY GOING BACK THE WAY WE CAME!

KILL HIM!
WHICH ONE?
EITHER!
PUNT!
OH. I'LL HAVE THAT.
WE APPEAR TO BE CORNERED.
CATWOMAN! ON THE GROUND, NOW!
DON'T SHOOT, OFFICER. I'M UNARMED.
TAK!

IF YOU CHOOSE TO TAKE A STAND NOW, IT WILL BE YOUR LAST, OFFICERS.
HELLO THERE, GENTLEBOYS.
TEN THOUSAND DOLLARS TO ANYONE WHO GETS ME OUT OF HERE NOW!
NOBODY MOVE!
ON THE FLOOR, NOW!
I MEAN IT!
THIS IS ABOUT TO BE QUITE FUN.
JOKER'S GOT A GUN! FALL BACK!
BLAM!
EVERYONE GET DOWN!
NO!
OR NOT.
TINK!

BOOOM!
WHAT THE HELL JUST HAPPENED?!
IT WASN'T THE JOKER. YOU BLEW UP CLAYFACE.
OH MY GOD. I KILLED THE WRONG GUY.
NO. HE'LL RE-FORM HIMSELF.
BUT WHERE IS THE JOKER?
SOME OF IT... IT WENT IN MY MOUTH.
FREEZE!
ALL RIGHT. YOU GOT US. AGAIN.
LOOK AT THAT.
I TOLD YOU SOMEONE STOLE MY--
SHUT THE @#$% UP!

GOTHAM CITY.
NOW THAT IT'S OVER WILL YOU EXPLAIN TO ME WHAT WE JUST DID?
BLAM! BLAM!
SKREEEECH!
OH, OF COURSE, MY DEAR. HOW THOUGHTLESS OF ME. IT ALL STARTS THAT NIGHT AT THE CLUB...
"IT BEGINS WITH THE RIDDLER TRYING TO WORK WITH ME AND MAKING ME AN OFFER I CAN REFUSE."
YOU AND I, WE DO THE SAME THING.
"I KNOW THIS. I WAS THERE FOR THIS PART, JOKER."
"THERE IS AN ART TO TELLING A GREAT JOKE, PUNCHLINE. THE SETUP IS THE MOST IMPORTANT PART.
"FROM THERE, I SET OUT TO DO IT ON MY OWN... WITH A LITTLE HELP."
MS. KYLE, I'D LIKE TO OFFER YOU A PARTNERSHIP.
WITH YOU?

"SO I HIRED CATWOMAN TO GET THE PIECES OF THE BOX FOR ME. AND SHE HIRED A TEAM TO DO IT FOR HER.
"AND EVEN WHEN YOUR PLANS ARE GOOD AND YOUR ADVERSARIES ARE MORONS, THE UNEXPECTED MUST BE EXPECTED.
SPLASH!
"THAT INCLUDES ROGUE CROCODILE MONSTER MEN.
"REMEMBER WHAT I SAID ABOUT DELEGATING TO DELEGATORS? IGNORE THAT. SOMETIMES IT'S IMPORTANT."
YOU WANT ME TO STEAL SOMETHING? ISN'T THAT YOUR THING?
YOU TAKE WHAT'S IN THE ROOM, SLADE. NO QUESTIONS ASKED.
WHY ARE YOU DOING THIS?
IT SEEMS TO BE MY JOB.

1016
GCPD
POLICE
BLAM!
SO YOU HIRED CATWOMAN TO HIRE DEATHSTROKE TO KIDNAP THE RIDDLER?
BRRROOOMM!
DEATHSTROKE IS A PARANOID WACKO. HE'D PROBABLY IMAGINE THAT I'D TRY TO SCREW HIM OVER...
"...SO I MADE SURE WHEN HE FINISHED MY JOB I SCREWED HIM OVER.
JUST WANTED TO LET YOU KNOW.
"PLUS I WANTED TO PROVE I WASN'T THE ONLY ONE WHO COULD STEAL STUFF IN THIS TOWN.
"BUT BETRAYAL IS A FASCINATING THING...
Nyieeek!
"...THE MORE OF IT YOU DO, THE MORE FUN IT BECOMES."
I'LL TAKE THE JOB. NOW SHUT UP. WE'RE GETTIN' TO THE BEST PART.

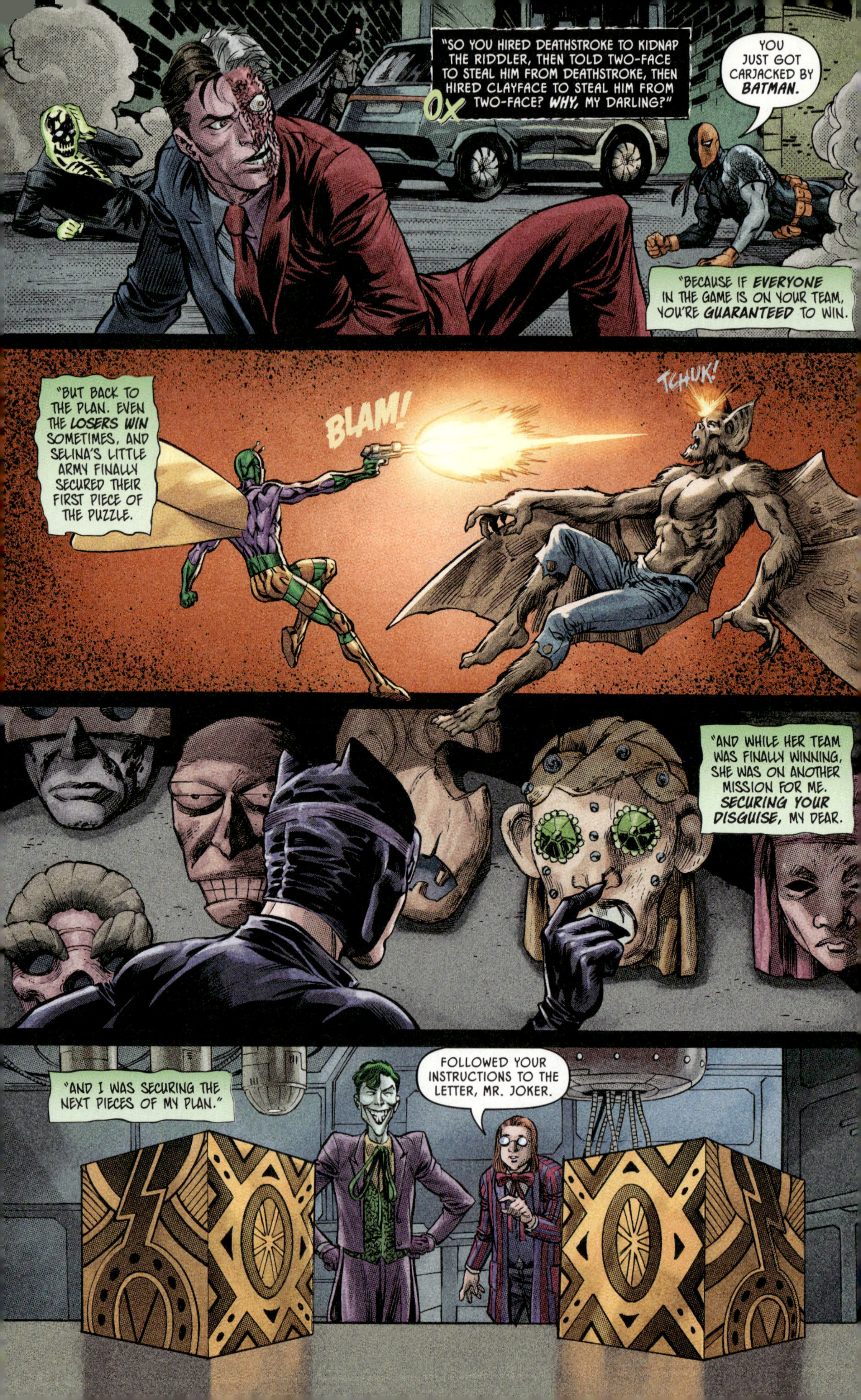
"SO YOU HIRED DEATHSTROKE TO KIDNAP THE RIDDLER, THEN TOLD TWO-FACE TO STEAL HIM FROM DEATHSTROKE, THEN HIRED CLAYFACE TO STEAL HIM FROM TWO-FACE? WHY, MY DARLING?"
OX
YOU JUST GOT CARJACKED BY BATMAN.
"BECAUSE IF EVERYONE IN THE GAME IS ON YOUR TEAM, YOU'RE GUARANTEED TO WIN.
"BUT BACK TO THE PLAN. EVEN THE LOSERS WIN SOMETIMES, AND SELINA'S LITTLE ARMY FINALLY SECURED THEIR FIRST PIECE OF THE PUZZLE.
BLAM!
TCHUK!
"AND WHILE HER TEAM WAS FINALLY WINNING, SHE WAS ON ANOTHER MISSION FOR ME. SECURING YOUR DISGUISE, MY DEAR.
"AND I WAS SECURING THE NEXT PIECES OF MY PLAN."
FOLLOWED YOUR INSTRUCTIONS TO THE LETTER, MR. JOKER.

"WITH MY REPLICAS IN HAND, I COULD FURTHER OBSCURE THE REAL PUZZLE FROM ITS PLAYERS."
YOU HAVE MY ATTENTION, FOR THE MOMENT, CLOWN.
"AND I SECURED EVEN MORE PIECES FOR MYSELF."
"AND WHILE THAT WAS HAPPENING, MY FAKE BATMAN CONTINUED TO DO MY BIDDING."
GIVE ME BACK MY HAT, YOU LOATHSOME--
"AND ALL THE WHILE THE GAME CONTINUED AND THE FOOLS DID THEIR PART."
BUDDA BUDDA BUDDA!
BOOM!

I'M OUT OF AMMO.
USE THIS.
WHY DIDN'T YOU GIVE ME THAT TO START?
YOU DIDN'T ASK. NOW MAY I CONTINUE?
"FROM HERE I JUST HAD ONE MORE LITTLE JOB FOR LITTLE OLD CATWOMAN.
"WITH ALL THE PIECES FINALLY ASSEMBLED...
"...EVERYONE CAME TOGETHER. RIDDLER'S TEAM TO MEET HIM, CATWOMAN'S TEAM TO MEET HER...
"...BUT INSTEAD ALL THEY GOT WAS ME...
"...ALMOST."

"AND YOU, IN YOUR LITTLE DISGUISE, HELPED ADD TO THE CHAOS.
BLAM! BLAM! BLAM!
YAIEEE!
"FROM THERE IT WAS JUST A MATTER OF DISSEMINATING THE FAKE BOXES THAT THAT CREEP TOYMAN MADE FOR ME.
"AND THEN EVERYTHING WAS IN PLACE. IT WAS TIME TO BEGIN THE END."
HELLO, POLICE? I JUST SAW A MAN IN A GREEN SUIT GET SHOT. COME QUICKLY.
"AND WE BEGAN COLLECTING THE PIECES..."
YOU! I WAS WORKING FOR YOU?!

"...AND CLEANING UP THE MESSES.
"I PAID FREEZE OFF WITH TWO-FACE'S LEDGER. I HAD ALREADY TAKEN OUT THE PAGE I'D NEED. I DIDN'T EXPECT HIM TO CARE.
"I GAVE CLAYFACE BACK THE HAT HE STOLE FROM THE MAD HATTER.
"AND THEN I GOT HIM DOWN TO A MORE CONVENIENT SIZE.
"AND THEN I JUST HAD ONE MORE SURPRISE, BUT IT WAS THE BEST ONE."
FEAR

THIS IS A REALLY CONFUSING STORY.
THAT'S WHAT MAKES IT FUN!
FWOOOSH!
WE GOT A BODY!
I SWEAR WE ALREADY SEARCHED THIS AREA BEFORE.
"I LEFT THE RIDDLER'S BODY FOR THE POLICE TO FIND."
YES, THERE ARE A LOT OF THEM. THEY SEEM QUITE SCARY.
"I ALSO TIPPED THEM OFF ABOUT THE NEXT PART...
"BECAUSE YOU CAN NEVER TRUST A COP IN THIS TOWN NOT TO SCREW IT ALL UP.
"AND AT THAT POINT IT WAS TIME TO CELEBRATE."

"I WAS ARRESTED.
"THEY TRIED TO FIGURE OUT MY LITTLE PLAN TO NO AVAIL.
BOOOOM!!
"THE LITTLE GIFTS TOYMAN MADE FOR ME WORKED LIKE A CHARM, ELIMINATING THE BASES OF ALL OF MY RIVALS AND DISTRACTING THE POLICE.
"THAT STUPID OFFICER BACHMAN WE FOUND IN TWO-FACE'S LEDGER BOOK WAS SUPPOSED TO DO THREE THINGS FOR US.
"THE FIRST WAS TRIGGER THE GAS ATTACK ON THE PRECINCT, BUT HE BLEW THAT AND CATWOMAN HAD TO INSTEAD."
HELLO, CLAYFACE.

"BACHMAN EVENTUALLY DID THE OTHER TWO PARTS OF HIS JOB RIGHT, THOUGH."
MA'AM, I NEED TO GET YOU OUT OF HERE. COME WITH ME.
"HE FOUND YOU IN YOUR DISGUISE."
I NEED THE JOKER TO COME WITH ME RIGHT NOW.
EVERYONE ELSE STAY PUT.
"AND HE FOUND ME IN MY CELL."
WHAT IS THAT?!
"AND I FOUND MY TICKET OUT."

TIME TO BECOME ME NOW, BASIL.
"WITH THE HATTER'S STOLEN MIND CONTROL TECHNOLOGY LODGED INSIDE HIM, HE HAD NO CHOICE."
TIME TO BECOME YOU NOW, JOKER.
"AND BACHMAN CAME THROUGH WITH THE FINAL THING I HIRED HIM FOR."
CCPD
YOU BROUGHT HIM BACK? WHY?!
PD
"AND WITH THE FAKE ME RETURNED TO THE CELL, THAT BOUGHT US ALL THE TIME WE NEEDED TO MAKE OUR ESCAPE...
...AND HERE WE ARE.

DAIRY KING
WHAT NOW?
I NEED TO CHANGE INTO SOMETHING MORE COMFORTABLE.
THAT'S BETTER. HOW DOES IT LOOK?
SO... WAS IT ALL WORTH IT?
DON'T ASK ME...
CLACK!
...IT WAS HIS IDEA!
RIGHT, EDDIE? THIS WAS ALL YOUR PLAN. YOU AND ME, ASSEMBLING THE MASTER ENGINE, RUNNING GOTHAM.
YOU THINK THIS WAS MY PLAN?! YOU KIDNAPPED ME! YOU TORTURED ME!
IT WORKED. EVERYONE ELSE IS LOCKED UP. IT'S JUST US NOW.

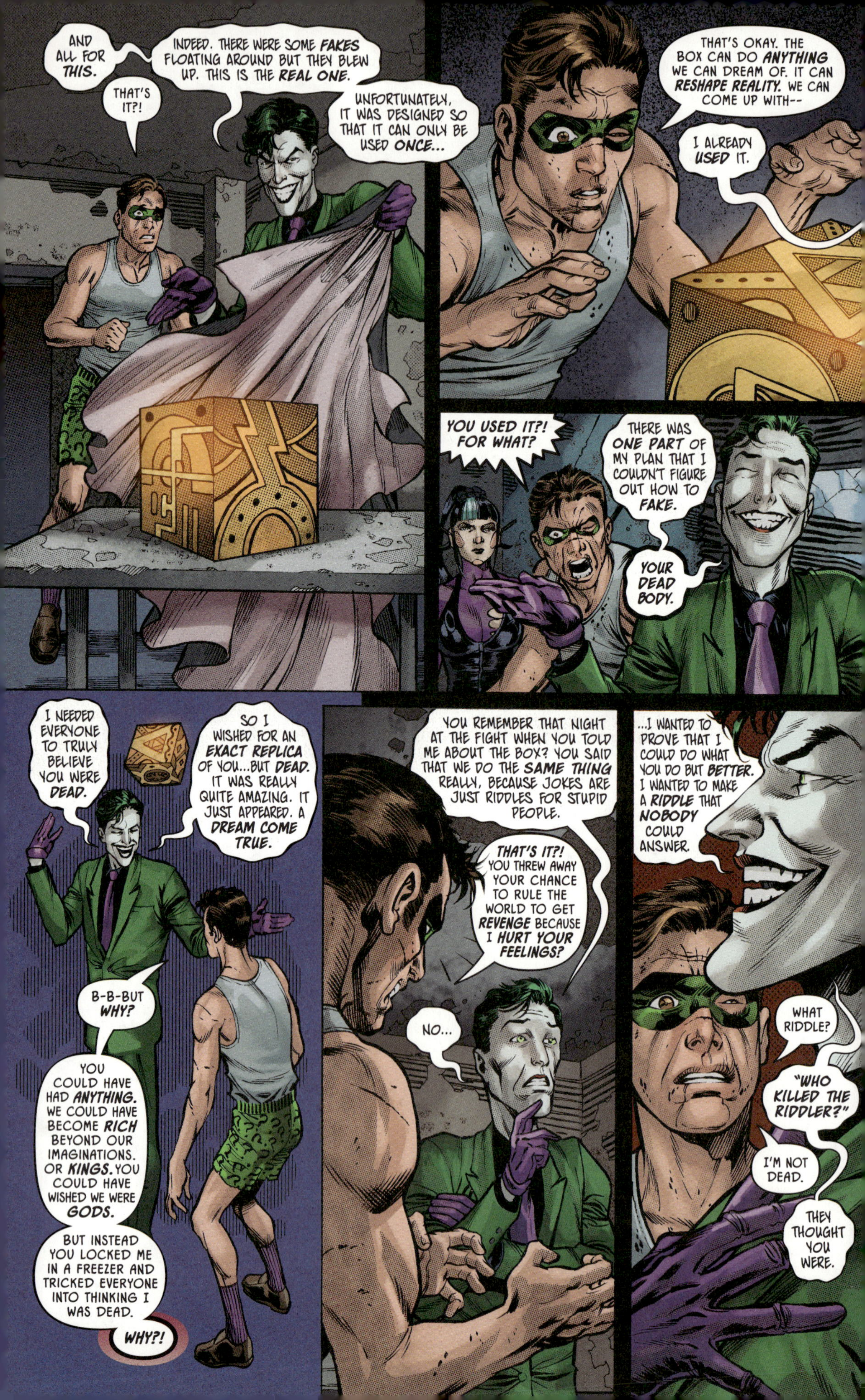
AND ALL FOR THIS.
INDEED. THERE WERE SOME FAKES FLOATING AROUND BUT THEY BLEW UP. THIS IS THE REAL ONE.
THAT'S IT?!
UNFORTUNATELY, IT WAS DESIGNED SO THAT IT CAN ONLY BE USED ONCE...
THAT'S OKAY. THE BOX CAN DO ANYTHING WE CAN DREAM OF. IT CAN RESHAPE REALITY. WE CAN COME UP WITH--
I ALREADY USED IT.
YOU USED IT?! FOR WHAT?
THERE WAS ONE PART OF MY PLAN THAT I COULDN'T FIGURE OUT HOW TO FAKE.
YOUR DEAD BODY.
I NEEDED EVERYONE TO TRULY BELIEVE YOU WERE DEAD.
SO I WISHED FOR AN EXACT REPLICA OF YOU...BUT DEAD. IT WAS REALLY QUITE AMAZING. IT JUST APPEARED. A DREAM COME TRUE.
B-B-BUT WHY?
YOU COULD HAVE HAD ANYTHING. WE COULD HAVE BECOME RICH BEYOND OUR IMAGINATIONS. OR KINGS. YOU COULD HAVE WISHED WE WERE GODS.
BUT INSTEAD YOU LOCKED ME IN A FREEZER AND TRICKED EVERYONE INTO THINKING I WAS DEAD.
WHY?!
YOU REMEMBER THAT NIGHT AT THE FIGHT WHEN YOU TOLD ME ABOUT THE BOX? YOU SAID THAT WE DO THE SAME THING REALLY, BECAUSE JOKES ARE JUST RIDDLES FOR STUPID PEOPLE.
THAT'S IT?! YOU THREW AWAY YOUR CHANCE TO RULE THE WORLD TO GET REVENGE BECAUSE I HURT YOUR FEELINGS?
NO...
...I WANTED TO PROVE THAT I COULD DO WHAT YOU DO BUT BETTER. I WANTED TO MAKE A RIDDLE THAT NOBODY COULD ANSWER.
WHAT RIDDLE?
"WHO KILLED THE RIDDLER?"
I'M NOT DEAD.
THEY THOUGHT YOU WERE.

SO I POSED THE RIDDLE TO THE WORLD, BUT THEY SOLVED IT.
I GIVE UP.
"WHO KILLED THE RIDDLER?"
"WHO CARES?"
THAT'S THE ANSWER. BUT EVERYBODY GOT IT. I GUESS YOU REALLY ARE BETTER AT THIS THAN ME, EDWARD.
YOU PSYCHOTIC @#$*&%--!
TEC!
EASY NOW. I'D HATE FOR YOU TO LOSE YOUR HEAD OVER SOMETHING LIKE THIS.
SO THIS WAS ALL SOME BIG JOKE?
SEE, I THOUGHT IT WAS A RIDDLE THIS WHOLE TIME. MAYBE THEY AREN'T SO DIFFERENT. OH WELL.
SEE YA AROUND, EDDIE.

LATER.
PSST JOKER.
OH, SELINA. WHAT A LOVELY SURPRISE.
IS IT A SURPRISE? BECAUSE YOU WERE SUPPOSED TO GET ME OUT. WE WERE PARTNERS, JOKER. THAT MEANS EVERYTHING YOU GET, I GET.
YES, WELL. NO NEED FOR ME TO GET YOU OUT BECAUSE YOU GOT YOURSELF OUT. AND AS YOU CAN SEE, I GOT NOTHING, BUT YOU ARE CERTAINLY WELCOME TO HALF OF IT.
I DO SEE. YOU USED ME, JOKER. YOU HAD ME DO YOUR DIRTY WORK AND YOU BETRAYED ME AT EVERY TURN.
WHAT CAN I SAY? I GUESS I'M A BAD PARTNER.
YOU ARE. THAT'S WHY I GOT OUT AND MADE A DEAL WITH A NEW PARTNER.
A NEW...?
HELLO, JOKER.
WAIT, I--
POW!
WHOK!
SOME PEOPLE DON'T APPRECIATE A GOOD JOKE. RIDDLE!

Variant Covers for

THE JOKER PRESENTS: A PUZZLEBOX

So many covers, so many suspects...

The Joker Presents: A Puzzlebox #1 variant cover by **CHRISTOPHER MOONEYHAM**

The Joker Presents: A Puzzlebox #1
variant cover by
JESÚS MERINO and ULISES ARREOLA

The Joker Presents: A Puzzlebox #1
variant cover by
RICCARDO FEDERICI

The Joker Presents: A Puzzlebox #1
retailer variant cover by TIAGO DA SILVA

The Joker Presents: A Puzzlebox #1
retailer variant cover by
MEGAN HUTCHINSON-CATES

The Joker Presents: A Puzzlebox #1
retailer variant cover by
DAVID CHOE

The Joker Presents: A Puzzlebox #1
retailer variant cover by **ZOE LACCHEI**

The Joker Presents: A Puzzlebox #1
retailer variant cover by **RYAN BROWN**

The Joker Presents: A Puzzlebox #2 variant cover by SHAWN CRYSTAL and JUAN DOE

The Joker Presents: A Puzzlebox #3
variant cover by **REILLY BROWN** and **JIM CHARALAMPIDIS**

The Joker Presents: A Puzzlebox #4
variant cover by **RYAN BROWN**

The Joker Presents: A Puzzlebox #5
variant cover by **DAVI GO**

The Joker Presents: A Puzzlebox #6
variant cover by **MIGUEL MENDONÇA** and **ENRICA EREN ANGIOLINI**

The Joker Presents: A Puzzlebox #7
variant cover by **REILLY BROWN** and **JIM CHARALAMPIDIS**

Puzzlebox and warehouse designs by **FREDDIE E. WILLIAMS II**

The Joker Presents: A Puzzlebox #1 layouts by JESÚS MERINO